Transfixing! What a joy to read Lloyd's eye-opening and satisfying collection of historical-fiction short stories. They filled in a lot of gaps in my understanding of what these settlers, from so many directions, went through as *They Came to the West*. I was deeply touched by the exchanges they had with the Natives, both friendly and hostile, whose lives they inexorably impacted. I was transported to the Old West and gripped by the nail-biting action sequences!

—Victoria Ouellette, Montana State University student

The book, *They Came to the West,* provides one with insights into just what those who came before us to this beautiful and wonderful part of the world found here.

—Karen Nowak, author of *Eye to Eye: The Language of Energy and Horse*

I've often wondered what the explorers and settlers of the West experienced and had to go through to get here. Lloyd's book gave me an idea of what it might have been like for them.

—Roy Runnings, retired union official

The gripping tales of the fictional characters in *They Came to the West* all gave this reader an image of the real life they found when faced with the harsh realities of those historic times and places.

—Abra Kair, caregiver

Hope you enjoy this!
Lloyd

THEY CAME TO THE WEST

Tales *of the* Migration *and* Settling *of the* American West *from the* Cave Man *to the* Industrial Revolution

LLOYD SHANKS

BOZEMAN, MONTANA

They Came to the West

Tales of the Migration and Settling of the American West from the Cave Man to the Industrial Revolution

Lloyd Shanks

Copyright © 2021 by Lloyd Shanks
and Mule Deer Press

Print ISBN: 979-8-5137059-7-0

Published by
MULE DEER PRESS
3426 Lemhi Trail Drive
Bozeman, Montana 59718

Printed in the United States of America

Editing, cover design, and typeset by Denis Ouellette

Dedication

This collection of historical fiction is dedicated to the memory of the late Doctor Alfred Louis Kroeber, who in 1911, was the head of the Anthropology Department at the University of California at Berkeley.

I recently met a man in Bozeman who was a retired professor from the University of California at Berkeley. He told me he had known Professor Alfred Kroeber before he died and that he was a fine gentleman. Based upon everything I have read about Doctor Kroeber, I had absolutely no doubts about that.

Alfred Kroeber's work with the last Yahi Native American, the subject of the last chapter in this book, was representative of a great dedication to the study of Native American cultures. His work deserves to be recognized and is well described, more accurately and in much more detail, in *The Story of Ishi—A Pictorial Chronology*, by Nancy Rockafellar, in the book *Ishi in Two Worlds*, by Theodora Kroeber, and in *The Last of His Kind*—both a documentary and the very dramatic Hollywood film by the same name.

—*Loyd Shanks, Bozeman, MT*

Contents

Preface

They Came to the West begins with a short and largely imaginative story of the very first people to inhabit the West coast of what is now the United States of America, and ends with a narrative about what happened to some descendants of those people centuries later. The book is a collection of ten stories about all sorts of people who came to the West from the four primary directions of the globe, and those characters represent a fair number of different ethnicities.

Each of the characters had their own reasons for coming. They may have been just seeking a better place than the one they came from, or a new way of life, and some of them found it. Some sought riches in the form of gold or silver. Not many found those kinds of riches, but many found a newer, and in other ways, a richer place to live for the rest of their lives.

All of the tales are historical fiction, based on some actual history, but are highly colored by the imagination of the author, who wishes he could have actually experienced some, but not all, of the many challenges those days presented.

Just what challenges? Maybe driving a wagon over a rutted trail leading to the Sierra Nevada Mountains, fur trapping, hunting big game (but not slaughtering any buffalo) and mining. Would I have had what was termed "the gumption" to have been a trapper, a "wild and wooly" mountain man, or a gold or silver miner back in those times?

Possibly, but I am sure that it would have been a far more difficult life than I've ever known. One can only imagine what it was actually like to live in those times!

Acknowledgements

This book would never have been published if not for the continued encouragement and help from my editor, Denis Ouellette, and from my daughter/ IT person, Karla Slyngstad. Denis' daughter, Vicky, contributed valuable insights along with her proofreading skills. Also I am grateful for the patience of my dear wife, Jan, as she sat through the hours I spent working on it.

For inspiration, I wish to thank Frank Mullen, Jr. for his work on *The Donner Party Chronicles*, which set the tone for the chapter, "The Wagon Trail West."

Introduction

The first people who came to the west were hunters, but they were also hunted. Their prey was the European bison and the Wooly Mammoth. Their predators were the cave bears and sabre tooth tigers. Many eons ago, these people originated in the middle of Africa. Then, over what took many centuries, they migrated to the north and east through the Middle East, Asia, and Russia.

After the continents had shifted and reformed and the world had tilted on its axis, glaciers formed, and the landscape was being carved and reshaped. The sea levels dropped, and modern geologists theorize that people were able to cross over a "land bridge" spanning what is now the Bering Sea to travel to a new home on the North American continent.

They traveled down the coast, passing a chain of many active volcanoes, stretching from what is now the State of Alaska down to northern California, a place that was much warmer than what any of them could remember. They found a land filled with new species of animals, lush plants and trees, and many lakes, rivers and streams full of fish. Life was good in their new home, and would remain that way for their descendants, until others in the world finally discovered it.

1 ❖ The Descendants

A Happy Day

Neesha, known by that name only to the members of the Yahi tribe and no others, was a happy young girl of fifteen. She had so many reasons to feel that way. On her way up Deer Creek to check the fish trap her mother had made for her, she spied a shiny reflection in a shallow pool at the base of a sandbar. After she waded across the creek to investigate, Neesha discovered it was one of the smooth rocks that shone like the sun! It was as large as her thumbnail and heavier than any rock of its size. Her mother could weave her a sinew cradle to hold it and a necklace for it that she could dye with blackberry juice, and she would wear her new treasure in three days when she was joined with Ohlan, her husband-to-be.

She would also be wearing the beautiful, elk-skin dress her mother had made for the ceremony. Mother had traded her finest, willow-branch basket for that skin just last week. A Coastal Miwok trader had brought the skin to the Yahi village from his home near the land by the sea. The trader was fascinated by the intricate weaving and multi-colored patterns on the finest basket he had ever seen and decided he had to have it and take it home to his wife. There was no doubt that Neesha's mother was the most skilled basket weaver the trader had ever come across in his seemingly endless travels.

Neesha knew what made the dress so beautiful was its soft, elk hair that was pure white with light brown spots. She thought that surely there was no dress that could even compare with this one in all of the several tribes that lived in the lands surrounding the mountain. It was strange that the mountain had recently started smoking again, after it had lain dormant for so many years. The tribe had also begun to hear it rumble and shake the earth. It was a fearsome experience for people unaccustomed to volcanic eruptions.

Mount Lassen, Northern California

The Yahi barely subsisted on a limited diet of venison. acorn and seed cakes, roots, bulbs and berries. Of course, the berries were only available in the Spring. The occasional trout, like the one Neesha hoped to find in her trap today, was a succulent treat for any of the lucky families that was able to trap one.

Neesha found a large trout in the cone-shaped fish basket that was shaped so a large fish that swam forward into it could not back out. The trout pleased Neesha because the large family, consisting of her father, mother, grandmother, brother and herself, often had hardly enough to satisfy them at any meal. She knew the addition of Ohlan to their family group would be a great benefit, because he was so proficient a hunter with his bow and arrows. Deer meat would be plentiful this Winter, but it was Spring now—a happier time with a bounty of berries, rabbits, ground squirrels, wild iris bulbs and this trout to eat.

The Joining of a Fine Couple

Neesha was the prettiest girl in the whole tribe. Most of the Yahi were short-statured people, on average, and not a very attractive people when compared to some of the other native tribes. In addition to being a skilled hunter, Ohlan was the tallest member of the Yana tribe, who lived just to the north of the Yahi. Both of those tributes had helped him win the hand of Neesha and the approval of her mother and father. Everyone believed any of the children born of this marriage would be wonderful additions to the rather small population of the Yahi tribe, which at that time, numbered less than three hundred.

Neesha's father was a toolmaker, not a hunter. So, the family had to rely on trading his tools and his wife's baskets for food. In hard times, when every scrap of food was being hoarded by all of the tribe, no one wanted to trade unless an obsidian knife blade had been broken or a food basket had holes worn through it, and that seldom occurred. So now, the addition of a skilled hunter to Neesha's family was a most welcome event. Ohlan's parents had only needed to present Neesha's family with a very modest offering in order to win the approval of Neesha's parents for the match.

The joining of these two young people would be a cause for celebration by the Yana. There would be dancing and feasting, provided enough food could be gathered in time. After the fires burned low, the tribe's two eldest story-tellers would take turns telling everyone the long tales of how the first people found this land to dwell in, near the mountain that had also been smoking those many moons ago. The oldest woman in the tribe would always tell how the first people came to the earth from a great hole in the ground. She told them that when their time above the earth was over, their souls would travel south to return to the earth through another hole.

Almost every member of the tribe, especially the elderly, would sigh and take solace in that thought. Their hard times on earth would be over when they traveled to live in that place beneath the earth where the soil stayed quite warm, even in the coldest Winter, and the joints in their fingers and toes would no longer ache. Also, every day they could soak their bodies in the pools of fragrant, hot and healing waters that sometimes bubbled up from the earth, instead of having to quickly wash themselves by splashing their bodies with the icy-cold waters flowing down Deer Creek from the mountains!

2 ❖ The Spaniard

He was born in Andalusia, the region at the southernmost tip of Spain, and his name was Antonio Francisco Alvarado de la Guerra. The de la Guerra (meaning *of the war*) was just an honorary title. One of his male ancestors was a cavalryman who had fought bravely defending his homeland against the hordes of attacking Moors, or "the barbarians," as the Spaniards referred to those aggressors, who traveled from North Africa to invade Spain in 711 AD.

The brave Spaniard had been well-mounted on an Andalusian war horse, wielded a sharp Damascus steel sword, and was later knighted by his King for his brave defense of the crown. In spite of the very best efforts of the rest of the defending Spanish army, the invaders overran the country. The Moors would occupy two-thirds of Spain for three-hundred years, at least half of it for one-hundred-and-sixty years, and finally, the prized Andalusian city of Granada for another two-hundred-and-forty-four years.

Since those initial battles, almost every male Alvarado had loyally served their country as officers in the Spanish Army, with the sole exceptions of Antonio and his father's brother Carlos. Antonio's mother had died in childbirth, and his father was required to depart for service in Mexico shortly after the birth, so he decided to leave the newborn infant in the care of a brother and his wife.

A Life at the Rancho

Uncle Carlos owned a large tract of land on the outskirts of Granada, where he raised Andalusian horses. As he grew older, Antonio learned how to properly care for the horses, to ride and eventually train the magnificent animals. Antonio also developed the skills necessary for calming the horses whenever they became unruly or frightened. One of the animals, a beautiful, creamy-white stallion, was extremely high strung, but Antonio and the animal formed a long-lasting bond that began when the colt was still nursing. When Carlos decided it was time the stallion needed to be trained, Antonio was given that task. In spite of Antonio's best efforts, the horse was always very unruly, especially when someone else tried to put a bit in his mouth and saddle him. Even though the horse would let Antonia ride him, either on a saddle or bareback, no one else was ever able to mount and ride what his Uncle Carlos called "the unruly beast!"

Each year an officer in the Spanish Army came to purchase a number of the Andalusians from Uncle Carlos for their Cavalry officers. The enlisted men were given "Spanish barbs" as their mounts. The barbs were descendants of the horses brought to Spain by the "barbarian" Moors. In later years, they would come to be called "Arabians." They were beautiful and strong animals that were well suited for the hot and dry conditions of Mexico. However, the barbs were nowhere near as strong as the Andalusians.

A Spanish Army captain came to purchase some mounts the year Antonio turned eighteen, and he said he wanted to buy the stallion the boy had grown to love. He intended to use it as a stud horse. Carlos tried to convince the man that he was making a mistake, because "the beast" would be too hard to transport. He also advised him that only Antonio could handle the animal. The captain informed Carlos,

"Then, we will employ the young man as a herd-master in charge of all the horses we are purchasing for transport by sailing vessel to Mexico, and this stallion will, of course, be one of them."

Antonio was thrilled by the offer of a position and a chance to sail across the ocean with his equine companion, and his uncle reluctantly decided he could go. He thought perhaps the youth would be reunited with his father in Mexico.

Off to Mexico and a New Life

Antonio was soon packed and mounted on the stallion he had named Compadre. He and a corporal were ordered to drive the herd to the port where the horses were to be boarded on a merchant sailing vessel bound for Mexico. After they reached the port, the horses were driven up a ramp with fenced sides onto the ship. Of course, Antonio had to lead Compadre with a rope halter to coax the stallion aboard. Once aboard, Antonio hoped the presence of Compadre would somewhat calm the rest of the nervous horses, but they were all still wide-eyed as their large hooves struck the wooden deck. The sound echoed in the below-deck compartment where the sailors would soon be berthed.

Antonio was informed that it would be necessary to secure the horses in canvas slings. They would be suspended from the below-deck crossbeams. If they were not secured in this manner, they might break a leg when the ship heeled as a result of the sea's motion. They would then have to be tossed overboard to the sharks that followed the ship and ate anything edible that was tossed overboard.

Of course, it was Compadre that was the hardest to secure and suspend on his sling. Each day, during the long voyage across the Atlantic Ocean, Antonio had to hand-feed and water all of the horses. He spent a lot of his spare time reassuring Compadre that all would soon be well.

When they reached the east coast of Mexico, the ship's Captain ordered the crew to "hove to" and then beach the vessel on an offshore sand bar at low tide. After all of the horses were hoisted in their slings up to the main deck, the crew was directed to remove the slings and push the reluctant animals over the side, so they could swim ashore.

Antonio was aghast, and asked the Captain if the animals might be attacked by sharks. The Captain told him that some of them would undoubtedly be attacked, but they might only lose one or two at the most. Antonio was not willing to see Compadre be one of these, so he decided to jump in with his horse and, if necessary, fight off any attacking sharks. Fortunately, he was spared that battle.

Once ashore, the horses were gathered together to be driven overland to Mexico City. The ship had already been brought alongside the dock by then, and the crew cheered as the small group of horses departed. They were quite pleased to be freed of the daily chore of cleaning the horse droppings off the floor of the "tween deck," as the seaman called it.

The journey from the coast to Mexico City was uneventful, with nothing more dramatic than some surly stares from some of the native inhabitants of the villages that Antonio and the Corporal drove the herd through. The two of them were pleased to finally arrive at the city and hopefully enjoy any of the comforts it had to offer. After they reported to the Comandante in charge of the Spanish Cavalry detachment, Antonio was advised that the Army no longer required his services. He was given the choice of either returning on the ship to Spain or enlisting in the Spanish Army and serving in Mexico. He chose the latter, because he wanted to stay with Compadre.

After being sworn in and supplied with a fancy uniform and riding boots, Antonio was shown to the enlisted men's quarters. He was given a wooden bed with a straw-filled mattress that he hoped was not already occupied with vermin. The other soldiers were anxious to hear news from Spain and asked about the voyage.

After a dinner of beans, corn and rice, they shared a bottle of red wine that the Corporal had hidden in his pack and managed to bring with him all the way from Granada. Their Sergeant advised them that it was the last wine they would enjoy for some time, because the next day they were being sent on an expedition to the north with orders to either capture or kill a small group of Chiricahua Apaches who had been terrorizing the population of Mexicans living in the territory North of Mexico City. The detachment would all be mounted and ordered to travel as long and as far as necessary to accomplish that difficult assignment.

Compadre had been so unruly that the Comandante decided the stallion was unsuitable for expanding their collection of Andalusians, and told his lieutenant, the administrative officer in charge of the company, that he wanted nothing more to do with the beast.

"Shoot him if you will," he said.

Then the Lieutenant, who was a compassionate man, advised Antonio, "If you want to save your beloved Compadre, you must accompany the detail who will be departing shortly on their mission to find the Apaches, and you will take that unruly beast as your mount!"

There was no doubt that this was the course of action Antonio would choose, and he went to pack his meager belongings.

The Lieutenant ordered his Supply Sergeant to issue a brand-new muzzle-loading carbine, pistol, powder, and lead balls, as well as a short saber to Antonio. Antonio knew nothing about the use of these weapons, but decided he could ask the Corporal to instruct him when they stopped for rest along the way. Unfortunately, that day never came because the troop was going to ride or walk their horses every day from dawn to nightfall in search of "los Indios."

Popocatépetl, "El Popo," active Mexican volcano

Bound for a Perilous Journey

The detachment left at sunrise. It numbered twenty-two mounted cavalrymen, consisting of the Lieutenant, a sergeant, a corporal and nineteen privates, including Antonio. The Lieutenant was mounted on an Andalusian and each of the enlisted men, with the exception of Antonio, rode Spanish barbs. There were ten pack mules loaded with all of the supplies necessary for their long venture into Indian territory.

The detachment left at dawn the next morning and were soon headed due west and passed to the south of a smoking volcano. Antonio had never even seen a volcano, but he had heard them described in great detail by the sailors who had seen some in Italy and Greece.

They rode west for two days before turning north in the middle of what would someday become the huge Mexican State of Sinaloa. After heading north for several days, they entered a much more desolate territory that the Lieutenant told them was the land of the Chiricahua Apache. After they entered the territory that would later become the State of Sonora, he said the soldiers should be aware that they were all putting their lives at risk. He said the Apache hated both the Mexicans and Spanish equally, and the Apaches' cruelty knew no equal whenever they took a prisoner. Everyone under his command should resolve themselves to put an end to their own life with their pistol or saber if it appeared they were about to be captured—being staked to an anthill, burned, or skinned alive would be infinitely more painful than a quick death by their own hands.

The Search for Los Indios

The Lieutenant made inquiries at many of the small hovels at the outskirts of the desert, as well as questioning each of the occasional wandering sheep or goat herder if they had seen any Indios recently. Whenever he made this inquiry most of the herders were reluctant to answer and would quickly shake their head no. However, one herder excitedly exclaimed, *"Los Indios? A la Norte!"* pointing toward the mountains far across what was an inhospitable desert.

When they heard this, some of the soldiers made the sign of the cross across their chest as they muttered "Dios mio" in an expression of their fear of what might await them. Many of them had heard tales of battles with the Apaches told by soldiers who straggled back to Mexico City, some with septic arrow wounds and all with a combination of torn clothing and many oozing skin punctures from poisonous mesquite-tree thorns.

Regardless of the risks, there was no way of slacking their orders from their Lieutenant. The men all knew this officer was a glory-seeker, and anxious to secure a Captaincy. One night the men quietly discussed this, and they all agreed that they would only follow the ambitious officer so far, and no farther. One soldier even commented that it would be a shame if some tragic accident should befall such a man in his ambitious zeal to drive the members of the detail to their certain destruction. After all, a huge rockfall, caused by the careless footstep of someone on a scouting detail on a bluff above, might be impossible to predict or prevent.

Entering the Sonora desert filled everyone with foreboding. It was obvious that even the Lieutenant was greatly concerned, although he tried hard not to show it. The scorching-hot days and near-freezing nights were taking a toll on all of the men. They were also running out of precious water, even though it had been strictly rationed since they entered the desert. Realizing Antonio had a much stronger horse than any of the other enlisted men, the Officer sent him and Compadre on a mission to scout the land ahead for any water hole that might be found near the foot of the rugged mountains that loomed far to the north.

That night, Antonio and Compadre headed towards the mountains with the hope that they would reach them by morning. Once there, he would give the horse its head and trust that he might possibly find some pool of water laying at the base of a rock cliff that still remained there after the last passing rain.

An Unfortunate Turn of Events

Around mid-morning, Compadre snorted and broke into a trot towards a craggy high outcropping of dark grey rock. He'd smelled a small pool of water in an indentation at the rocky base of the cliff. Antonio found that the water was quite warm, but it tasted so good! Just as he was about to dip his whole head into the pool to cool it, a small rock dropped into the other side of the pool and Antonio looked up and saw a group of Apaches armed with bows and arrows. Then, four others with lances popped up from behind rocks on both the right and left. It was apparent that his luck had run out, because both his carbine and pistol could only fire one shot each before Antonio would be peppered with arrows or run through with lances. It appeared that none of the Apaches had horses, so the only hope that Antonio had was that the Apaches might be satisfied to take Compadre and spare his life.

The four Apaches carrying lances approached Antonio with their weapons pointed right at his chest. The Spaniard decided to drop all of his weapons, and the four Apaches immediately grabbed for them. However, because there were only three weapons, an altercation broke out over who got one. Antonio thought that this might present an opportunity to escape with his horse, but when he saw that all of the Apache's bows were still aimed directly at him, he abandoned the idea. When his uniform jacket was being pulled from his back, he tried to resist but was quickly overpowered and thrown to the ground. Then his boots and pants were quickly pulled off, and in a matter of seconds he was stripped completely naked.

Antonio fully expected to be staked down and left to bake in the sun until he died, but the Apaches attention suddenly shifted to Compadre. Another fight broke out between the four natives to determine which of them would end up with the horse.

Compadre reared up and struck the closest two fighters with his forehooves and then charged through the melee toward Antonio. As the horse passed by him, Antonio grabbed the horse's flowing mane, swung aboard, and urged the stallion forward until it reached its full stride.

They left the four startled natives behind. The Apaches on the rock shot their arrows, but none of them hit either the horse or Antonio, and he had made good his escape. Because he was riding naked, it was not long until he had several sores rubbed through the skin on his buttocks, but that was a small price to pay for his freedom!

Lost in a Wasteland

All that day, Antonio searched the horizon in vain for some sight of the Calvary detachment. At the time of his escape, he'd paid little attention to the direction Compadre took as the horse galloped away. The noon sun was high in the sky and Antonio had no way to determine his directions, which compounded the problem of attempting to head back in the general location of the detail. Of course, by now it was quite likely they had moved on far from there.

As the sun began to set it was possible to determine the four points of the compass. There was a low range of black hills to the north, but the distance to them was hard to estimate. Antonio thought that if he rode through the whole night, he might likely reach the hills by sunrise. His bare skin was badly sunburned and traveling at night would help him recover. He'd already cut and peeled some aloe plant leaves, and the slick, moist inner pulp relieved a bit of his discomfort.

Antonio rode half the night and kept falling asleep. Afraid of falling off the horse, he decided to try to find a place to sleep a bit. Off to his right, there was a black rock bluff that looked like it might provide a place to take a temporary rest. When he reached the site, Antonio noticed that there was an overhang, and the bright light from full moon revealed a pile of fine pale-colored soil at its base that had been piled against the bluff by the fierce desert winds that often blew across this wide expanse of desert. After dismounting, he walked over to the foot of the bluff and scooped out enough soil beneath the overhanging rock to fashion a hollow he could slide into and take a short nap. The sand was still warm and within moments, he fell into a deep sleep.

What started as a restful nap, turned into a nightmare! It began with the distant howls of a pack of black, Mexican wolves. The howls grew louder, as the pack approached. The howls turned into fierce growls and snarls. Then, Compadre whinnied and galloped off into the night.

Antonio woke with a start and learned the nightmare had turned into a reality. The ground around his makeshift bed was almost covered with wolf tracks. The deep hoofprints leading north was evidence that Compadre had fled in an attempt to outrun the hungry attackers. Even though Andalusians were large, strong horses, they were not as fast as the lighter Spanish Barbs, and Compadre would probably not have been be able to outrun a fast pack of wolves. Antonio feared that his life might be the very next one taken by the pack of vicious predators. Even though he knew it would be better to wait until the next evening, the need to move away from this location was overwhelming.

Moving Towards the Coast of a New Land

It was time to head west, toward some high mountains. The wind was somewhat cooler as it began

sweeping across the desert from the distant ocean to the west. Two hours later storm clouds began forming over the mountains in the distance, and the low rumble of thunder could be heard together with the crackle of lightning. It back lit the clouds, as it struck from one to another in the dark sky. There was a smell of rain in the air, so Antonio knew that before too long he might be able to quench his thirst with cool rainwater, as long as he could find a place where it would pool. He turned and began climbing the rocks at the face of the bluff.

On the top of the black, volcanic stone bluff, there were some shallow pockets in the surface of the stone that might soon be filled to the brim with rainwater. This would have been an ideal place to stay for a rest, if it wasn't for that wolf pack that might return that night for their next meal. Soon, the rainstorm hit and filled the indentations on the bluff. After drinking all of the water from the indentations that he could, Antonio started toward the west.

Two days later, Antonio finally reached the mouth of the Colorado River. After he was refreshed and bathed, his new direction of travel was toward the Mojave Desert. After finally reaching it, he learned that it was not only as inhospitable as the Sonora Desert, but it also contained more hazardous creatures than he had previously encountered. The deadliest was the sidewinder rattlesnake, but at least a rattlesnake gave someone much more warning than the gila monsters in the Sonora! Coyotes replaced the black wolves, but at least the breed seemed to have a strong fear of man and constituted no real threat.

Antonio was near the point of death from starvation. He had obtained some moisture from the pulp of cactus plants, but had nothing to eat for the past fourteen days. In an appeal to God, the poor soul vowed that if he could somehow be spared, he would become a servant of both the Catholic Church as well as any peaceful native peoples who he found to inhabit the region he was headed towards. Of course, he would first have to survive the Mojave—both the desert by that name and the savage Mojave Indians who inhabited the harshest environment imaginable.

His relief came in the form of a huge rattlesnake, longer and thicker than his arm. It gave the usual rattle warning as Antonio noisily stumbled through the thick brush as he headed towards a rainwater wash. The Spaniard picked up a huge stone and threw it down on the sidewinder's head, which fortunately killed it instantly. The snake had a total of twenty-two rattles, as evidence of a long, undisturbed life. Antonio skinned and ate it raw, since he had no way to make a fire. He

topped off his meal with a dessert of the soft, red fruit from a cactus called a "prickly pear" after he had removed the spines from the outer skin by rubbing it briskly with a rough stone. Of course, it was nowhere near as tasty as the real pears he'd enjoyed in Spain, but it seemed like a gift from God. That meal provided him with enough strength to continue his long journey west.

Many days later, the Spanish Mission of San Diego came into view, and Antonio staggered, naked and badly sunburned, into the plaza at the front of the mission. Both the priest and his friars tending their gardens were quite shocked at the sight of the unfortunate soul who approached. They were amazed to hear that he had walked barefoot—practically from the Sonora desert to the shores of the Pacific Ocean! The exhausted soldier was taken into the Mission, washed and soothed with an application of aloe, given a wrap of woven cotton and a meal of goat cheese and tortillas, as well as a bed and mattress stuffed with soft, seaside grass.

Mission San Diego

After hearing the details of how he'd survived the Apaches and two deserts, his vow to God, and learning that he was a good Christian, the priest decided to allow Antonio to become a friar. The priest said his services were not required in San Diego, but they should be sorely needed in the north, where new missions were being built and several Native tribes were presently being converted to Christianity.

Antonio was given two friar's robes, a donkey, and all the necessary provisions he would need for his travels to the northern Missions in the new Spanish territory of California, named after a fictitious island ruled by Queen Califia.

El Camino Real

During his travels to the north, the priests and friars at one mission after another welcomed Antonio. He told the fascinating tale of his travels from Mexico City and his survival to the residents at the Spanish missions in Santa Barbara, Carmel, Monterey, San Jose, and San Francisco, all of which were connected by *El Camino Real* (the Royal Road). When he reached the Mission named for Saint Francis, he was told this was the end of El Camino Real. However, the next new Mission was being built in San Rafael, on the north side of San Francisco Bay, and his services would surely be welcomed there. In order to reach that Mission, it would be necessary to travel back to Mission San Jose, located on the south end of the bay, and then travel north along the east shore of the bay and across the straits where a great wide river entered the bay from the northeast.

Antonio was advised to leave the donkey there and was given some trade goods to present to the friendly Ohlone Indios in exchange for one of their small round boats made of tule reeds that he could use to ferry himself across the straits. After crossing, he needed to walk towards the west until he reached the northwestern edge of the bay and then turn southward to Mount Tamalpais, the highest peak on the peninsula. If he needed any more detailed directions to reach Mission San Rafael, he could ask any one of the members of the local tribe of Spanish-speaking Coastal Miwoks. Many members of the Miwok tribe in that vicinity were working for the Missionaries, so any youngster Antonio might encounter might have a father, mother, brother, or even an older sister working there.

Antonio made his way south on El Camino Real to the Mission at San Jose and was invited to spend the night there as an honored guest of the priest. The next morning, he worked his way north along the east side of the bay until he reached an Ohlone village. There were no reed boats there, but Antonio was directed, by sign language, to travel north to the place the fast flowing river met the large, salt-water bay.

It took a full day to locate the Ohlone fishing village. It had many racks for drying the fish with reddish-orange flesh and a number of reed boats lying along the shore of the wide river. Antonio signed that he wanted to trade for a boat, but when he displayed the goods the friars at the Mission gave him in trade for the donkey, the Ohlone men declined to trade one of their handmade reed boats. None of their boats were large enough to transport two, so asking to be ferried across the river was out of the question. Antonio reasoned that if the Ohlone men could build a reed boat, then he should be able to build one too, but there was no sign of any of those tule reeds growing along the shoreline.

When he had just about given up the idea of crossing the river, an old Ohlone man approached. He was dragging an ancient reed boat, and signed that he was willing to trade his boat for the trade goods Antonio had brought. The reeds were bone dry, but the old craft might be able to make one more voyage, and the trade was completed.

Across the Swiftly Moving Straits

A small gathering of Ohlone saw a frail reed boat carrying a white man in Missionaries' clothing being launched the next morning. The fast-moving river that flowed into the northeast entrance of San Francisco Bay immediately caught it. The current swept the small craft toward the wide mouth of the bay. Antonio paddled as hard as he could in an attempt to turn and head for the north shore, but it was to no avail.

The reed boat was being swept past another, much narrower river that flowed into the bay from the north. There was what appeared to be the tip of a peninsula, or perhaps an island, on the west side of that river, but it was quite obvious that it could not be reached in spite of Antonio's frantic paddling. Eventually, the current became much weaker as the river waters mixed with those of the huge bay. There was quite a strong wind blowing from the southwest, and it started the old boat, which now appeared to be starting to come apart, toward the northern Bayshore.

About one hundred yards from the shoreline, the old craft began to finally disintegrate, and Antonio decided he could easily swim that short distance to shore. But, after he slipped over the side, Antonio learned that the murky water was only about two feet deep, so he was able to wade the rest of the distance to the muddy shoreline. The next one-hundred yards of muddy shoreline was covered with a thick growth of marsh grass that was difficult to walk through, but the thick grass did help clean some of the gray mud and slime off his calves and ankles.

When the exhausted young man reached a trail through the marsh grass that ran east and west along the first high ground he came to, he turned and headed west. The trail was well worn and cut deep into the gray soil. It was obviously very old and likely had been worn down by the passage of many of the Indios in the region.

After several hours of hiking, Antonio came to the east bank of a shallow tidal creek that flowed from the north in a serpentine track. There was a thick growth of tule reeds on both banks of the meandering creek, and Antonio now knew where the Ohlone came to get the reeds to build their unique boats. After fighting his way through the thick growth of reeds on the east side and wading across the shallow creek, Antonio pushed through the reeds on the west bank. It was then that the large mountain that he had been told to head for came into view. That was the landmark that he needed to head for Mission San Rafael.

Serving the Comandante Instead of God

The mission was still under construction and, after he was welcomed and fed, Antonio was advised that he would be put in charge of the Indios that would be producing baked adobe bricks for the walls of the new Mission. He was told he could take charge of a crew of Coastal Miwoks who had already been clearing the site for the Mission. Antonio advised that he had no knowledge when it came to supervising construction, and he was only skilled as a horse handler and trainer. He was told that he might find work elsewhere because that was an extraordinary skill.

A nobleman who lived in a fine villa in the nearby village of Sonoma was willing to employ him because he owned a number of large, creamy-white colored horses he was attempting to train. Antonio soon learned that the man was a Spanish General named Mariano de Vallejo *(Vah-yay-ho)*. Vallejo was the Co-mandante of the Spanish territory of California.

The Comandante owned several Andalusian horses that he wanted trained for the purpose of exhibiting them in a display of what was called "dressage." This involved training the steeds to walk in an almost ballet-dancer fashion, to bow and do acrobatic jumps. Antonio told the General that he was certain that he could do that, and he was hired.

Many years later, after the *Norte Americanos* won a brief war, called the Bear Flag Revolt, with the Span-ish occupiers, a town located at the juncture of the two rivers Antonio had once floated across was named Vallejo in memory of the General who had welcomed the *Norte Americanos* to California and was not opposed to their taking the territory away from the Spaniards.

Antonio spent the rest of his years working for General Vallejo. He never revealed that he had once been enlisted in the Spanish Army. He had absolutely no intention of returning to a way of life in the service of the Spanish King and Queen like all those other Alvarado men had devoted their lives to.

3 ❖ The Mountain Men

Mountain Men were brave souls who went west to make their fortunes (or so they hoped) by trapping beaver. In the early 1800s, men's top hats made of beaver skin were the height of fashion in England and the eastern United States.

The first Mountain Man was John Colter, who was one of the members of the Lewis and Clark Expedition, which had been formed to explore the lands west of the Missouri River. He left the party to trap beaver in Montana when they were returning from their two-year exploration. He was captured by the Blackfoot Indians near the three rivers that formed the headwaters of the Missouri in Montana, but he managed to escape, naked and unarmed, by outrunning members of the tribe.

Sacagawea with William Clark and Meriwether Lewis

Mountain men Jim Bridger, Davey Crockett, and Kit Carson all found rivers teeming with beaver, and soon Fur Trading Companies were formed. They sponsored groups of trappers who came to harvest the pelts of beaver and other fur-bearing animals. They would buy the furs for cash, less than the cost of all of the supplies they'd supplied the trappers with at the start of the season. It was rare that a Mountain Man got rich trapping for a Trading Company.

The Trading Companies also traded with many Native American tribes for any furs they'd trapped and not used for their own clothing. The natives had no use for the white man's money, but wanted the knifes, axes, pots and pans, used single-shot muzzle-loading rifles, powder, lead bullets, and tobacco that Trading Companies brought with them each year. The natives always wanted to trade for whiskey. Frequently the Trading Companies supplied them with a low-quality whiskey that was commonly laced with red pepper and wood alcohol. This concoction was what Native Americans often referred to as "firewater."

How It Started

Sam Whitney was employed by one of the Missouri fur-trading companies as a warehouseman before he decided to become a "mountain man." Each season a huge amount of trade goods and supplies, called "necessities" by the trappers, were stored in Saint Louis, Missouri. The supplies arrived on a paddlewheel riverboat and were warehoused until Spring when they were loaded onto wagons for transport West.

Sam met several trappers who had just returned from a very successful season of harvesting beaver pelts from the rivers and streams to the west. One trapper had described in glowing terms the beautiful country as clean and free of a common illness called "the fever."

However, he warned Sam that it was a wise mountain man who heeded the warning, "If the 'injuns' don't get you, then a grizzly just might!"

He pointed out that Grizzly bears sometime confronted a lone mountain man who'd had the misfortune of wandering into the bear's territory. It was difficult to kill that large a bear with a single-shot rifle. If one shot failed to kill it, then it might be necessary to finish off the attacking beast with a knife or an axe. The trapper told Sam that more than one Mountain Man that he personally knew had been severely bitten and clawed during an encounter with an angry grizzly.

Sam knew it was not exactly pleasant to be a mountain man, because they had to endure a hard, lonely and dangerous way of life. It was not the kind of life that should be undertaken lightly, but he decided to give it a try. His previous attempt at trapping some beavers on the river close to home last season was actually a bitter disappointment. He'd trapped so few beaver that he almost gave up the idea of trapping altogether, but decided to give it one more try. Next Spring, he'd try to join a party of more experienced trappers and get his stake from an established Fur Trading Company.

A Second Chance

Spring arrived and Jim found a group of trappers who said they could always use an extra man. They all drew the supplies they needed from the company. The men grumbled among themselves because they knew the prices they would be charged, when their fur pelts were being sold to the Trading Company would be higher than they would have paid the merchants along River Street. But few of them had saved the money they'd need to buy them in St. Louis. Also, the Trading Company would transport those supplies to the country to the west where they were sorely needed.

Even if the trappers had been able to buy their own supplies, they would have to transport them all the way to the trapping grounds on a backpack or drag the load behind them on a travois. None of the trappers were willing to do that, so they resigned themselves to have the inflated prices for what they called their "necessities" deducted from their earnings. Sam briefly considered using all of the cash from the sale of his meager bounty from his first year of trapping, but learned it was hardly enough to purchase everything he needed for his second attempt. Of course, if he did no better at trapping this season, he'd be in debt to the Trading Company at the end of fall.

Sam was sure he needed a better weapon to replace the old rifle he had been given by his father when he left home. One of the trappers told him that the best rifle he could buy would be a .50 caliber Kentucky rifle. They were one of the finest rifles made, and he even happened to know an old trapper who had decided to give up the hard life, settle down in town, and was willing to sell his. Sam was able to meet the man's asking price, and was left with some cash to spare, so he decided to buy both of the men a drink or two. The three of them spent the rest of the afternoon at the town's only Saloon. When they staggered out that evening, all three were "feelin' no pain."

The next morning Sam had his regrets. It wasn't because he'd spent the last of his money. Since he really had no interest in gambling, he probably would have little use for it after they left for the trapping expedition. His biggest regret centered on how bad his head ached after yesterday's drunken celebration. He slowly walked to the old trapper's cabin to pick up his rifle. Because he no longer had any use for them, the old man gave Sam his gun cleaning supplies, two cans of black powder, a supply of lead and a bullet mold, plus a full tin of percussion caps. Sam was very grateful for the old trapper's generosity, and told him so. That gift was certainly important because, after yesterday's expenditures for drinks, he had no money left to purchase the supplies he'd need to use the rifle he'd bought just yesterday.

On Their Way West

The group of trappers set out the next morning, following the wagon train full of supplies. Most of the men were on foot, but several of them had mules that they rode without saddles. They said their mounts would be used as pack animals when they had bales of beaver pelts to transport to wherever the Trading Company had selected for their annual collection point.

Their trek west continued for several days without any incidents. However, on the fourth day one of their group spotted some smoke signals atop a nearby ridge. Sam thought that today might be the first day he'd need to put his rifle to use. Of course, it was only a single-shot weapon.

A number of the trappers carried pistols stuck in their waistbands for that important second shot, but buying a pistol on credit from the Trading Company stores would be quite costly. A lower cost secondary weapon might provide just the needed defense, and a well-crafted tomahawk seemed a much more affordable choice. Besides being less costly, it was a fine well-made defense weapon.

The company man explained, "That's a good choice! A whack on the head or neck will put a man down almost as fast as a rifle ball, and then you can always take as many whacks as necessary."

"So, are you worried about them smoke signals, son?" one of the other Trading Company men asked. "Them smokes is probably just some Kaws signaling their thieving brothers to tell 'em we're comin' with goods they can steal. But if they're Kiowas, then we might have a real fight on our hands!"

There was no attack that day, but that night Sam slept lightly, with his hand clenched around his precious rifle, fearing that the Kaws might steal it. The mountain men arrived at the east bank of the Arkansas River the following day. All of the supplies and trade goods had to be unloaded and put aboard some flatboats that were tied to the trees along the banks.

It was necessary for the men to push the flatboats upstream with long poles against a strong downstream current. It was the time of the "Spring thaw" and the icy brown waters were clogged with cakes of ice and floating brush and trees that had been uprooted. The men were told to keep a sharp watch for any "snags"—old logs that no longer floated and were lodged under water. Some of these could only be spotted by looking for the eddies that swirled around their tops at the river's surface.

The Trade

The men poling the three flatboats were able to make their way upriver without hitting any snags. When they were busy negotiating one of the "oxbow" bends in the river, one of the men on the lead flatboat cried out, "Injuns on the right bank!"

As his flatboat rounded the bend, Sam saw a group of Natives mounted on painted ponies. Each of them had a few black feathers tucked in their headbands. The Natives were waving and appeared to be friendly.

One of the trappers said, "Those are Crows, and they are friendly. It appears they want to trade."

Most of the trappers had brought tobacco and glass or chinaware beads and buttons for trading, so the flatboats were beached and the trading began. Sam hadn't brought any items for trade, but one native came over to him and pointed at Sam's rifle. Sam clutched the weapon across his chest and signed that he would not trade it. The native pointed at the breach of his rifle and held up the thumb and first finger of one hand as if he held a small object in them.

"He needs some caps!" one of the crewmen exclaimed.

Sam had a full tin of percussion caps and knew he could spare some of them to trade. The native brought out a beautiful handmade knife sheath made of tanned elk hide that was decorated with dyed porcupine quills. Sam knew it would be perfect for his skinning knife and offered ten percussion caps in exchange. The Native held up five more fingers. The Native offered the knife sheath, and Sam got out five more caps, making it a total of fifteen, which was what he thought he could easily spare. After the trading was complete, and the boats were pushed off the bank, they were on their way and headed back upstream.

Eventually a Trading Company man pointed out a clearing where they needed to stop and unload the supplies. He explained that this is where they would meet for a rendezvous in the Fall. He told the group that it would be important to keep a count of the number of days and be back here in no more than one hundred days. Any longer might result in the risk of the group having to stay for the entire Winter, since the Winter "ice-up" of the river could come as early as mid-October. All of the trackers agreed to keep a close count of the days until they would meet again.

One trapper approached Sam and told him that the best trapping sites could be found near the "headwaters." This was where the three rivers recently discovered by the Lewis and Clark expedition were joined together to form the Missouri—a place now called Three Forks, Montana. It was then that Sam decided he needed to team up with a more experienced trapper, if he wanted to become a *real* mountain man.

Sam asked the man if he was interested in teaming up and heading there together. The two of them started backpacking the supplies they'd need upriver. It took them several days, and after they had reached the location where the three rivers joined, they agreed that one of them should take half the supplies and go up one river, and the other go up the other. If there were no beaver lodges on one river, there was always the chance that the third might have a good number of beaver families living on it.

Sam was making his way up the Madison River when he encountered a female grizzly bear with two cubs. Not wanting to disturb the mother bear and risk an attack, he backed away and decided to cut across country to the Gallatin River.

A Fight to the Death

Halfway to the river, Sam came out of a grove of aspen trees and saw a Brave mounted on a paint horse about forty yards from the edge of the grove. The native held a lance at his side, and his face was blackened with soot. Sam sensed that he was in grave danger. Without any warning, the brave kicked his pony and it started galloping forward. The sharpened point of the wood lance was aimed directly at Sam's chest, so he had almost no time to react. Sam grabbed his rifle and raised it to his shoulder, but didn't have time to cock the hammer and take aim at the onrushing savage. His only option was to step aside to let the horse and rider pass and swing the rifle like a club.

Sam wasn't able to get the rifle high enough to reach the rider's head, but he did manage to strike his neck and knock him off the horse as it passed by. The brave sprang to his feet, and just as Sam got the rifle pointed toward him to take a shot, the native grabbed its long barrel and pulled it so hard that Sam had to let go in order to keep from being dragged within reach of the native. Sam wished he'd been able to grab the tomahawk he'd selected from the supply wagon, but fortunately he did have the skinning knife in its new scabbard on his belt. He had the knife out in an instant, and just as the native leapt forward Sam thrust it toward him, piercing his abdomen. In less than a minute the fight was over.

It would have been fortunate to find and catch the horse, but it was nowhere in sight. Fearing the animal would return to the brave's camp and others of his tribe would be able to backtrack it to this site, Sam gathered up his belongings and made a retreat back to the Missouri. If he failed to catch up to the flatboats, he'd just have to walk all the way back to St. Louis. He'd made his mind up that the hard life of a Mountain Man was not for him!

Return to St. Louis

Sam returned to St. Louis and learned that another man had filled his position as a warehouseman at the Trading Company. However, he was asked to start working as a teamster, hauling supplies from the docks at the riverside to the warehouse and then transporting them to the groups of mountain men each year.

Years later, when the so-called Indian Wars were underway, he signed on as a Cavalry Scout for the U.S. Army. He and three Pawnee Scouts were tracking a group of "hostiles," (braves who'd chosen to leave the reservation) when the four scouts were ambushed by a group twice their number. As they all headed for cover, Sam was hit in the back with an arrow. When he dropped from his saddle to the ground, he knew the wound was mortal. So, as a brave approached with a drawn knife, Sam took out his pistol and put a bullet in his own head, rather than run the risk of being scalped alive.

4 ❖ The Wagon Trail West

In the mid-eighteen-hundreds, even prior to the discovery of gold in 1849, there began a wave of westward migration across the United States. The ultimate goal was to reach the west coast of this new country, so "on our way to California" (or Oregon) was a common theme of those who chose to make the arduous journey across the country. Their wagons followed the tracks of those who had gone before them, all taking part in the drama that was involved in what in those days was termed "manifest destiny." This was a "politically correct" term for settlers pushing westward to inhabit the lands that, at that time, were occupied solely by Native Americas and Mexicans.

By the 1860s, the wagon tracks over the long trail leading west were carved so deeply that they can still be seen in places on the land between the Missouri River and the Sierra Nevada mountains. Some of these ruts, carved by the steel rims on the wooden wagon wheels, were so deep that a man could sit at the top and his feet wouldn't touch the bottom.

Looking Westward

Thomas Marshall, a resident of Springfield, Illinois, had long dreamed of traveling with his wife Martha to begin a new life in California. They were friends of James and Margaret Reed, who had departed two years earlier and ended up joining the ill-fated Donner Party that had to spend the Winter of 1846–1847 trapped in the high Sierras. After numerous newspaper and magazine articles had told stories of how many of the party had starved to death, Martha was extremely reluctant to undertake the journey. Tom explained that the wagon trains were taking a new route that avoided the difficult pass over the mountains now named for the Donner's. The easier route was over Carson Pass, which followed the Carson River south of the arduous route taken by the Donner Party.

It was 1850, and just a year earlier, Tom's brother James had discovered placer (or loose) gold, in the river that ran alongside his sawmill in Coloma, California. Now, thousands were traveling west to seek their fortunes by mining, but Tom was not interested in becoming a gold seeker. Mining was even harder than carpentry. Tom had built many houses and barns around Springfield, and at age 48, he knew he would not be able to continue doing so much longer. He planned to make furniture when they got to California. He was skilled enough to build fine furniture and had built all of theirs. He was sure there would be a demand for furniture by the hundreds of people who were migrating there. When James had written, he described the mild climate, plentiful oak trees, and rich farmland around Sacramento. He had also told them how he heard the wide deserts of Utah and Nevada were littered with discarded furniture that had to be abandoned there to spare the lives of oxen that were dying of thirst while trying to pull the heavily loaded wagons.

Martha had insisted that if they traveled to the west, they would take her widowed mother along. The Reeds had done this with their enlarged wagon that accommodated Mrs. Reeds' needs. Tom decided he could cut a doorway in the side of their wagon and build some steps that would give the old woman a way to enter it without climbing. He could even make her a small, single bed using the lightest wood available. He used dried cottonwood for the bed and a tiny cabinet with a drawer to store the patent medicine she used for a hacking cough. Like most of those "patent medicine" concoctions, it contained a good percentage of alcohol. Martha and he decided they would sleep in a tent in canvas sleeping bags, in which they could place a wool blanket. Martha made the three of them some thick mattress pads she filled with cotton batting.

They sold their house and all of their furniture to buy a fine new wagon built by the Studebaker brothers in South Bend, Indiana. They also bought six oxen as well as two mules for he and Martha to ride. Tom had found a young local man who wanted to go to California and had agreed to be their teamster. After cutting in a side door, building the steps and the bed and cabinet for his mother-in-law, Tom started buying and loading all the supplies needed for the trip. Besides their bedding and clothing, the rest of the wagon would be packed full of foodstuffs. They packed numerous sacks of beans, dried peas and corn, cornmeal, flour, salt and sugar, several wood kegs filled with salt pork and smoked bacon, and two tins of lard. There were also two large wooden barrels for water–one mounted on each side of the wagon, and a bucket of axle grease hung under the wagon bed.

Tom also built two small chicken hutches on one side of the wagon with wood lath, so they might be able to have some fresh eggs on the journey. That was at least as long as the caged fowl managed to last. On the other side, he mounted a sturdily braced shelf and frame to hold his heavy carpenters' tool chest filled with all the hand tools he needed for creating furniture when they reached California.

They planned to set off as soon as the Spring rains stopped, and the road leading to Independence, Missouri was dry enough to take their heavy wagon over. Once there, they should be able to join a wagon train that would follow the deep wagon ruts across the Indian Territory and into the west. The wagon trail leading to California wound across the "Indian Territory" that is now the states of Kansas, Nebraska, Wyoming, Utah, Idaho, and Nevada. They hoped to be on their way by the first week of May, and to reach Independence about a week later.

When they finally arrived, they found that Independence was teeming with people and activity. The town's blacksmiths were busy making iron shoes for the oxen teams and the saloons and dry-goods stores were filled with every kind of person. There were the mountain men, traders, barmen, gamblers, lawmen, prostitutes, and local residents, as well as the potential members of the many wagon trains that were being assembled. There were some Indians in town, but they were only some poor members of the Kaw tribe, whose territory was just to the west of the south fork of the Missouri River.

Tom made his way to one of the dry-goods stores to buy a rifle and ammunition. He was advised that the best muzzle-loading rifle available—the one everyone wanted—was a Hawken. It, plus some coffee, took the last of their funds. Tom was certain that the rifle was worth it, and he thought he could probably sell it for more than he paid for it once they reached California.

Tom decided that the wagon train they joined should be one that was well provisioned, since he was sure they could not spare any of the food they were able to pack in their wagon. There were quite a number of wagon trains being made up, but few of the trainmasters had taken an inventory of the supplies being taken by its members. Finally, Tom met a wagon train master who had. He was a burly Scot named McCleary, and he showed Tom a detailed list of everyone and everything the fifty-five parties who had joined carried with them. McCleary's list indicated that the train already contained the following:

57 wagons
87 fighting men, 53 women and 99 children
52,635 pounds of flour and cornmeal
34,280 pounds of bacon and salt pork
959 pounds of gunpowder
2,300 pounds of lead
130 rifles and shotguns and 84 pistols
675 head of oxen and cattle and 135 horses

Tom shared his list of supplies with McCleary and was told he was welcome to join their wagon train.

Disturbing Thoughts

They planned to set off the next day, which was the twelfth of May, but first Tom and Martha took time to visit the local Historical Museum that had just been built. There, in a glass case, was a page from a Springfield, Illinois newspaper, containing the following advertisement:

WESTWARD HO!
FOR OREGON AND CALIFORNIA

WHO WANTS TO GO TO CALIFORNIA WITHOUT COSTING THEM ANYTHING? AS MANY AS EIGHT YOUNG MEN OF GOOD CHARACTER WHO CAN DRIVE AN OX TEAM WILL BE ACCOMMODATED BY GENTLEMEN WHO WILL LEAVE THIS VICINITY ABOUT THE FIRST OF APRIL. COME ON, BOYS! YOU CAN HAVE AS MUCH LAND AS YOU WANT WITHOUT COSTING YOU ANYTHING. THE GOVERNMENT OF CALIFORNIA GIVES LARGE TRACTS OF LAND TO HER SONS WHO HAVE TO MOVE THERE.

—GEORGE DONNER, WAGON TRAIN CAPTAIN & LEADER

In the same case was a copy of a letter written by Tamsen Donner, dated May 11, 1846, which had been written by her in Independence. Its contents read:

I am seated on the grass, in the midst of our tent, to say a few words to my dearest only sister. Tomorrow we leave to go to California, the Bay of San Francisco. It is a four-month trip. We have three wagons furnished with food and clothing and such. I am willing to go, and I have no doubt it will be an advantage to our children and to us.

Tom and Martha were moved to tears knowing that on October 31st of 1846, almost six months after that letter was written, the Donner family was trapped in the mountains by a four-day blizzard, and both Tamsen and her husband George would not be able to escape with their lives—even though their five daughters were all rescued the following Spring. The Reeds, James and Margaret and their two sons and two daughters had also managed to somehow survive.

Westward Ho!

The wagon train set forth the next day as planned, but they got a late start. It took quite a while for everyone to finish cooking and eating their breakfast and to complete their final packing for their departure. There was also a lot of time lost while everyone jockeyed their wagons for position in the train. Nobody wanted to be on the back end, but Tom and Martha's wagon was the last one in line because they had been the last party to arrive and join up. This bothered Tom because in the event of an attack by any Indians from the rear, his wagon would be the first one struck. It later became clear that there were a couple of other problems that plagued those at the rear of the train.

Everyone agreed there would be no stopping for lunch, since everyone had a large, cooked breakfast. Anybody who was hungry could snack on fried corn-bread balls, which the southerners called "hush puppies." Because of their late start they only traveled six miles the first day, and McCleary addressed the crowd at dinner and told them they would have to do much better in the days ahead, or they would be left behind. No one wanted to hear that, and all agreed that they would do their best from that day forward.

They woke up to a driving rain the following morning. No one bothered to try to build a cooking fire and satisfied themselves with eating whatever was at hand from their dry stores. They got started early, and soon all of the fifty-seven wagons ahead of Tom and Martha's were turning the trail into deep ruts filled with oozing mud. Now Tom knew one of the reasons nobody wanted to be in the rear of the train.

In spite of the heavy rain and deep mud, they made ten miles that day before they found a spot for the train to circle and camp. There were a number of deadfall tree trunks that the men hacked into to get enough dry wood to start some large fires that the women could cook over. Once they got the fires blazing even the dampest wood could be thrown into the fires and everyone could dry off alongside the large blazes.

The rain had stopped by the next morning. That was a relief, because some of the canvas wagon covers had been thoroughly soaked through around their seams, and folks thought that they would not keep out much more rain. McCleary announced that later that day, they would be fording the Big Blue River, less than twenty miles West of their starting point in Independence. This would be the first river crossing for several of the wagon team drivers. McCleary told them that because many other wagon trains before them had successfully made this crossing, as well as numerous other crossings, they shouldn't be troubling themselves about it. Still, his words did little to ease the minds of several of the families.

They reached the Big Blue later that afternoon. McCleary said the flow of water was faster than usual because of the rain the day before. It was also so muddy that the bottom could not be seen. McCleary said the best way to safely get across was to enter and cross as quickly as possible, and that no one should stop once their teams had entered. The oxen would have to be whipped if necessary, and no one should spare the beasts if they wanted to get the wagons, passengers and goods across safely. Any wagon stopped in the river was liable to be turned over by the fast-flowing current.

The line of wagons started to cross. The shouts of the men and the crack of whips could be heard by the others moving up in line to take their turn at crossing. As the sixteenth wagon reached the middle of the river, one of two lead oxen stumbled and dropped into the water, pulling the other into the fast-moving current. After the other oxen were dragged into the stream, the wagon began to tip. Those men whose wagons had already crossed jumped into the river and rushed to the down-stream side of the tipping wagon and pushed with all their might. Fortunately, the wagon was stabilized, and the oxen team was able to regain their footing. When the team was back in line, they were able to start moving across the river. The rest of the train was able to cross without further incidents.

Not far past the river crossing, the train came to the edge of a great expanse of tall grassland that stretched all the way to a range of hills on the horizon. McCleary advised that it would be wise to stop for the

day and allow the oxen to rest and feed. One of the men told him that he could see a small herd of buffalo in the distance and several others agreed to ride ahead with him and slay one to roast for dinner that night. Others agreed to cut some small willow trees near the river and construct a travois to drag the buffalo back to camp.

That night all enjoyed some delicious buffalo meat. For many of them, it was the first buffalo they had ever tasted. Before they had finished, a group of half a dozen mounted Indians approached the wagons.

There was some alarm among the wagon train members, but the Indians made it clear that they were not hostile. McCleary said they were from the Shawnee tribe, and he used his hands to sign that they were welcome to join in the feast. Each of the six took large portions of the meat and sat down to eat. After they finished their meat, one of the wives offered them servings of cornbread, which they really enjoyed. McCleary offered them a generous handful of cut tobacco and bid them farewell. After they had left, McCleary told the group that he hoped every group of Indians they encountered would be as friendly, but he had serious doubts that they would be that lucky.

Follow the Blue

McCleary told the group that the next day they would be traveling along the northern banks of the Big Blue River, and would be crossing it again. He advised them that by the time they reached the crossing, the flow should be less, as long as it did not rain again.

The sky was clear of clouds when they started moving toward the river, and it didn't seem that rain would be likely. The wagon trail was starting to dry out, but there were plenty of fresh oxen tracks in the middle of the trail that told them they were not far behind another wagon train that had set off the day before them.

After cooking breakfast and packing up the train got an early start. The trail followed the river, which was flanked by numerous willows and cottonwood trees, and they crossed the The Big Blue without any incidents. To the north of them lay the wide expanse of tall grass prairie, the likes of which none of them—except McCleary—had ever seen. A fresh wind from the west had picked up, and the tall green grass undulated in waves like water on the surface of a large lake.

There was a larger herd of bufallo in the distance, and one of the men rode out and shot one for camp meat. The train was now deep into what would some-day become the State of Kansas, and McCleary advised that they were close to Pawnee hunting grounds. For-tunately, after the one buffalo was shot, the herd stam-peded to the north and passed from sight. So, the chances of coming in contact with a Pawnee hunting party were slim. Nevertheless, many of the men kept a sharp eye on the grassland north of them, since the Pawnee tribe was known to resent the crossing of their hunting grounds by the many wagon trains. Many of the natives believed the deep wagon trail would disturb the migration of the buffalo that they hunted to provide the main source of food for their tribe.

James Wilson, the young man who had agreed to drive the oxen for Tom and Martha, proved to be equal to the task. Of course, Tom always helped him yoke and hitch up the teams each morning and unyoke them in the evening. The oxen and cattle has been doing well so far. The prairie grasses provided the teams with ample nourishment, and the river water suited them well. Each of the families boiled the river water to replenish the supply of drinking water stored in the wooden barrels. Those stores of water would be crucial for the days when they were not near any rivers or springs. The hens had started laying some eggs again, so Tom, Martha, her mother and James were able to enjoy some of them each morning.

That evening, following dinner, someone brought out a fiddle. Quite soon afterwards everyone was enjoying the dancing that followed. James was a fine-looking lad, and before long it was clear that he had attracted the eldest and prettiest daughter of an Irish family of five, all of which had red hair. Tom told Martha they made a fine couple, and James would do well to propose before the journey was over. Martha replied, "We'll see." Tom quietly answered, "Yes we will, my dear."

The next morning, McCleary told the group they would be crossing the Little Blue that afternoon and would be traveling on the south side of the river heading toward The Platte River and Chimney Rock. The sky was still clear, but the breeze had passed. By mid-morning it was uncomfortably hot. The trail was completely dried out, and the wagons ahead were kicking up dust that started to bother those at the tail end of the train.

Martha's mother started to complain that the dust had made her cough worse and she broke out a fresh bottle of her patent medicine. Tom figured that the bottle would not last the day and the rest of them would not last the trip. However, as long as her supply did, it kept her quiet and helped her nap each afternoon.

Late that afternoon, they spied a line of willows that told them they were coming close to the Platte. Also, off in the distance there was a small dark-colored speck that McCleary pointed out as Chimney Rock.

"We'll be there by tomorrow afternoon," he declared, "but we will be crossing the platte first thing tomorrow morning. It's wide, but not that deep, and you will have no trouble at all." Tom hoped not, but he wondered what Indian tribe's territory they would be entering next and what trouble that might bring.

That evening, shortly after circling the wagons for the night encampment, a group of half a dozen Pawnees rode up, and McCleary went out to meet them. When he came back, he said they had come to demand a steer in return for the bufallo that had been killed, and the man who had shot the animal should be the one who should give it to them.

Jason Roberts, who had shot the animal declared, "That's nonsense. They don't own those bufallo we saw. The herds roam free on the prairie and they belong to no one!"

McCleary replied "You shot it on the Pawnee's hunting grounds so the tribe considers that buffalo was theirs. So, you had best give up the steer. After we cross the Platte we will be in the territory of the Cheyenne. So, you had best refrain from hunting any bufallo out there. If you should be caught hunting by the Cheyenne, you will not be fortunate enough to settle up with a steer."

Across the Platte

Shortly after they set out the next morning, they arrived at the south bank of the Platte River. McCleary announced, "Here we are at the Platte. This river flows all the way from the foot of the Rocky Mountains and feeds the Missouri. It's not deep, but the bottom is quite sandy. Keep your oxen moving and you won't get bogged down. After we cross the river, we will be in Cheyenne Territory. This tribe has been hostile towards other wagon trains, so we may be subject to attack if they come across us. We can circle the wagons for our defense as soon as any hostiles are spotted. If they're wearing their war paint, we will be in for a battle. If any of you men have brought an extra rifle or a pistol, make sure your oldest son or your wife knows how to load the weapon. Then, after you have fired a shot, you can pass the weapon back to them and be given a reloaded one. This will greatly increase our firepower. Use the wagons for cover to avoid being hit with their arrows, and concentrate your fire on any Indian that rides toward the circle of wagons. Some braves will hurl lances, but they are easier to see coming, so you may be able to dodge aside and avoid being struck by one."

They followed the trail west along the north side of the Platte RIver as the day passed. Late that afternoon, McCleary, who had been scouting the trail ahead for a place to camp that night, came riding back with his horse at a full gallop. He called for a halt of the train and told the driver of the lead wagon he had spotted a number of mounted Cheyenne braves who, after they spotted him, rode off quickly to the north. "Pick up the pace, and pass the word to follow me to a spot where the river has cut a high bank on this side. We can circle the wagons with one side of the circle on that bank. If we are attacked, it will be only from one side. Even if some do come at us from the river, it will be easy for those with pistols to pick them off as they come over the top of the bank."

They arrived at the spot McCleary had found for their camp and circled the wagons as the sun was setting. The women started their evening meal, while all the men readied themselves for a possible attack. No Indians arrived, and soon darkness fell over the plain to the north. When they were eating their meal in silence, contemplating a possible attack, some yips and howls could be heard.

"Prairie wolves," someone said. "No, those are Indian signal cries. We need to ready ourselves for an attack at dawn!" McCleary said. "Won't they attack at night?" someone asked.

"No, they don't. They believe that if they are killed their spirits need to have light to find their way to the happy hunting grounds. Sometimes, they cut out the eyes of their dead enemies because they believe their spirits cannot find their way, and they will be destined to wander the earth for all time." "That's horrible!" a woman cried out.

"So is the scalping of the dead, but that's what they do, so all of you be ready to fight for your lives tomorrow!" McCleary emphatically replied.

An Attack at Dawn

Not many of them slept well that night, and all of them were up well before dawn. The women cooked biscuits and salt pork and took it to the men who were standing at the ready by the circled wagons. As the prairie lightened before sunrise, the dark shapes of horses could be seen about five hundred yards to the north of them. Then, as the sun rose the Indians mounted their ponies and began to ride at a gallop toward the wagon train. McCleary shouted, "They are coming! Get all of your weapons ready, and loaders stand behind your men—but take care to stay behind the cover of the wagons!"

The Indians rode toward the train in a line, with the foremost all armed with bows. The mounted men behind them carried wooden lances. McCleary told the group of defenders, "After the first have shot their arrows and you have taken your first shots, the ones with lances will follow. Get your second weapon. If you don't have one, duck behind the wagon and reload as quickly as you can!" Tom had practiced reloading his Hawken many times during the journey. He hoped he had done so enough to reload in time to take a second shot at the Indians atacking with lances.

There were close to one hundred attackers and most were armed with bow and arrows. The first volley of shots from the wagon train killed only a few of the passing line of Indians.

McCleary shouted, "Shoot the horses first. Then get ready to pick off the rider with your second shot. Those with lances should be easier targets as they ride toward the wagons!"

His advice was heeded, and before long there were a number of unmounted Indians being shot at. The Indians who had thrown their lances and were not wounded rode back to pick up survivors who had lain down for cover behind their horses that had been shot and killed.

As the attack continued, more Indians and their horses were killed, and soon all of the attackers rode off to the north. McCleary advised that after attending to the few men who had been wounded, they should break camp quickly and move westward in case the Indians returned with greater numbers. They traveled farther that day than any of the previous ones, spurred on by the thought of another attack. The shape of Chimney Rock was sighted in the middle of the flat prairie and grew larger by the hour. "We will reach it by early light tomorrow," McCleary declared.

That night the mood in the camp was somber as a result of the attack that morning. McCleary tried to cheer them up by telling them it was a very good sign that a second attack had not followed the first, and they would probably not be attacked again by the Northern Cheyenne. He did not mention that the next tribe ahead of them to the north, the Sioux, were also considered to be hostile.

Arrival at Chimney Rock

The next day around noon, the train reached Chimney Rock, in the heart of "Indian territory, and it was an amazing spectacle. The hill behind it, and the huge, dark-colored rock, almost as high as a sailing ship's mast, rose up from the middle of the flat plains. There were names and dates carved into the rock, and a number of the men started searching for some tools that would enable them to add theirs. One man even asked Tom whether he would lend him one of his chisels, but Tom quickly refused his request.

McCleary was furious. "Here now! There's absolutely no time for such foolishness! Look to the west!" There, on the horizon, was a large cloud of dust. "That is either a large group of riders or a buffalo stampede. It might be a large party of Sioux or Northern Cheyenne, so we had best prepare ourselves for another attack. Circle the wagons around at once!"

After circling the wagons and getting their weapons ready, the party waited. It was quite a long time before a large group of riders could be sighted. McCleary had taken out a brass spyglass and declared the riders were coming in a column of fours and carried a flag. "Those are horse soldiers! The cavalry is coming to protect us!"

When they finally arrived, the Army scouts riding ahead of the column advised that this was a regiment of the First Cavalry, under the command of a Captain Benton. When the troop rode up, the Captain announced that they had been dispatched to protect the many wagon trains that were crossing the prairie on their way to California.

"We'll do this by keeping up roving patrols that are intent on keeping any Indians to the north of the trail, rather than riding along with any one of the trains." He advised McCleary that they should continue on their way, as there had been no sight of any Indians since they had started their patrol.

In a few minutes the wagon train resumed their trek westward as the troopers headed back to the scene of the Cheyenne attack. The day was hot and the trail was quite dusty. Tom and Martha rode alongside the wagon and listened to her mother complain about her choking cough as she got one of the remaining bottles of patent medicine out of the cabinet Tom had made for her.

"I don't know why I let you two convince me to come on this dreadful journey. I should have stayed home where I was comfortable, instead of having to be trapped in this stifling wagon and breathing all this dust!"

The soldiers had advised that there would be no sources of water between there and Fort Laramie, in the Wyoming Territory, which was still several days of travel ahead of them. This was the first time they would be relying on all of the water in the barrels on their journey. Tom was glad he had mounted two of them on the sides of their wagon. Some wagons only had one barrel, and this was a mistake that would present a very serious problem in the days to come. They were able to reach Fort Laramie without any further problems and there was well water available there, so all were able to refill their barrels.

There were a number of Indians camped outside the Fort. McCleary was informed that they were peaceful and many of them were related to their Pawnee Scouts. He was also advised to make sure they stuck to the main trail ahead of them. The troopers had heard of a man named Hastings that had talked the Donner Party into taking a so-called shortcut, leading south into the Wasatch Mountains. It took the party an extra month to cut their own trail through brush and tree filled canyons, which led to their ill-fated attempt at crossing the Sierra Nevada mountains in late October.

The trail beyond Fort Laramie headed northwest to skirt around the highest part of the Rocky Mountains that were looming on the skyline ahead of them. They had been advised that the next fort on the trail was Fort Hall and west, located to the west of where the wagon trail branched northwest toward Oregon and southwest toward California. As far as any possible attacks by Indians was concerned, they were told the Blackfeet tribe posed the main threat. That tribe was hostile to everyone, even neighboring tribes.

Fort Hall (replica), Pocatello, Idaho

Arrival at Fort Hall

Two weeks later they reached Fort Hall. They had not been attacked by any of the Blackfeet tribe, and learned that the tribe had been too busy raiding the Sioux to the east of the territory that the Blackfeet considered exclusively their own. The area west of Fort Hall was occupied by the Shoshone, a tribe that was not considered hostile, except when they were fending off an attack from the Blackfeet.

However, shortly after their wagon train arrived at the Fort, the Commandant informed McCleary that there had recently been an incident involving the Shoshones that had caused them to attack the wagon train just ahead of them. He explained, "Some idiot fired at a Shoshone hunting party and killed one of the braves! A few hours later, a war party attacked the train and killed three innocents. I dispatched three mounted companies that are pursuing the tribe to the north. I am hopeful that they will not present a threat to you folks, unless they circle and back toward you."

McCleary explained to the group that the trail heading northwest from there would be more difficult than what they have traversed so far. Just to the west, the trail headed up into the mountains, and the grade was so steep they would need to double-team each wagon to get them over the pass. Then the trail headed south through a valley with feed and water for their oxen. They needed to rest them well because they also faced a long trek through the desert located beyond a river that sinks into the sands. He said that much of the ground water in the desert has been saturated with alkali, and will poison anything that drinks it. There were skeletal remains scattered about of some of the poor souls who tried drinking the alkali water.

After resting a day at Fort Hall, they set out on the trail again. They saw the Rocky Mountain range they were told about, looming in the distance. The range appeared to be much steeper than any of them had ever seen.

Rocky Mountain Range

McCleary told the group these mountains were comparable to the Sierra Nevada range that they would have to cross as they entered California. The trail ahead was filled with numerous rock washes that were the result of heavy rains and snowmelt from the mountains.

Several of the spokes on wagon wheels were broken in the process of crossing these washes, and the train had to stop while wheels were replaced with spares the wagons carried. While this was undertaken, the oxen hooves were all inspected to see if any of their steel shoes needed to be replaced. Spare shoes were soon nailed on to replace each of the missing and worn out ones.

One wagon tongue had developed a large crack, and Tom got out his tools and fashioned a splint to re-inforce it. The tongue would need to be replaced as soon as they found a tree ahead that was suitable for fashioning a new one. Presently, they were in an area where only sagebrush was growing. While the temporary repair was being made, a number of the other wagon owners removed wheels and re-greased the axles on their wagons.

All this time, some of the other men were on the alert for any sightings of hostile Shoshone tribesmen. Someone spotted smoke signals to the north just as they were getting underway, and McCleary told them "Those signals mean there are at least two groups of Shoshone. I'd venture a guess that the tribe divided its numbers, and one group peeled off to the left and the other to the right, and both will backtrack to the rear of the pursuing Cavalry. We will not be able to out-distance them, especially when we reach the mountains and have to double-team the oxen to get each wagon up the steep grade. Also, we will need to find a good spot not far ahead for a defense like we did at the attack by the riverbank. I will ride ahead and scout for one."

The train continued all day without catching up with McCleary. As the sun was just about to sink below the mountains ahead of them, he appeared and advised there was a box canyon a half-mile ahead near the foot of the mountains.

"Alright! If we circle the wagons near the entrance, we will not have to worry about an attack from the rear. We can put all the animals inside the canyon and not have to worry about them being driven off during an attack."

They finished setting up just before dark and enjoyed an evening meal. As they settled around the fires for a final cup of coffee, yips were heard in the brush land in the distance. McCleary said he was unsure if those were real coyotes or Indian signals. Either way, we should stay alert for a possible attack at dawn. Not many slept very soundly that night, in spite of the hard day of work they had experienced. Sentries were posted at the front of the canyon while breakfast was being cooked, and some of the women took them biscuits and salt pork and cups of strong coffee they could consume at their posts.

Before long, there were alarms raised after a group of riders approached. McCleary said they were Shoshone, and they were each mounted on beautiful Appaloosa horses dappled with spots. Some were gray with black spots, some black with white spots and the leader was mounted on a horse that was reddish-brown with light grey spots. Their leader was dressed in a beautiful white buckskin shirt and leggings, decorated with multi-colored spots like the horses. He carried a lance with eagle feathers, and the rest of the riders carried bows. They were wearing war paint, and appeared menacing as they rode up but did not launch an attack. Their leader rode up to the sentries, but none of them raised their weapons when he did.

The leader stopped his horse a few yards short of them and stared them down. He then raised his lance with its tip pointed to the sky, turned and whooped toward his men. He pointed his lance back toward the way they had come. McCleary came up to the sentries and exclaimed, "The leader was just testing you to see if you would shoot at them. The first man to raise his rifle would have been run through with his lance. You were all wise to hold your fire, and they have decided to let us pass through their territory in peace. Let's pack up and leave before that other group they were signaling arrives. They might not be as understanding!"

Head for the Hills

The next morning McCleary told everyone the hills ahead were less than a day's ride away. "We will have an early stop this afternoon and give the animals a rest before we start up the next morning. It will take us a full day to get all the wagons up to the top." When they reached the foot of what they'd thought were just hills, they discovered they were actually another steep mountain range.

The necessary double-teaming of the oxen was done as quickly as possible, with the oxen team from the second wagon quickly unhitched and brought up and hitched in front of the first. Then, as that wagon started up the steep grade, McCleary instructed the men in the third and fourth wagons to double their teams as soon as the second wagon had been double-teamed and started up the hill. It was slow going up the steep grade. The oxen's hooves were slipping in the loose soil that had been dug up by all the oxen from wagon trains that had gone before.

When they stopped to let the animals rest a bit, the wagon brakes had to be applied to stop the heavy wagon from rolling backwards and dragging the teams with it back down the hill. It was necessary to use whips and shouts in order to get the oxen moving again, and the occupants also had to push on the rear wheels with all their might to help get them starting to roll.

There were numerous exposed rocks in the trail. The wagon drivers tried to steer around them in order to protect the wheels, but one particularly large rock near the top of the ridge could not be avoided and a loud crack could be heard as one of the wagons came down off the top of one. The driver shouted, "Now that beats all. I've probably broken a wheel." However, the wagon kept on without faltering.

When they reached the top, it was discovered that the wagon's rear axle was cracked. The driver pulled the wagon to one side so as not to block the way for the next ones coming up, and the driver unhooked the extra oxen team and led it back down the hill. Once he heard that, Tom started searching for a tree that might serve for a new axle. It would take a couple hours to fashion one, and he'd need help from others to install it. He located a large mountain ash and began to chop it down. After removing the limbs and cutting a length long enough for the axle, Tom started dragging it up the hill. It was quite a task, and after a quarter of an hour, he was quite winded. He asked the next wagon driver that came by if he could tie the heavy tree trunk to the back end of his wagon and the driver agreed.

When Tom and Martha's wagon reached the top, McCleary told the two wagon drivers that the rest of the train had continued ahead to find a place to spend the night. "You can shape the axle here and rest up before putting it on and then join up with the train around mid-morning tomorrow."

That night McCleary told the group, "We will stop here for one day to allow the two wagons we left behind to catch up, and let the animals feed and rest up for the ordeal ahead. There are several long grades ahead of us before we reach the Sierra Nevada and only several streams where we can water the stock before we reach the Humboldt River."

The way down the mountains was a relief after that difficult climb up. There were several small meadows of green grass for the animals to feed on. They made a stop to replace a few steel wagon wheel tires. McCleary told the men to make sure to carefully check the condition of their wagons, since there would be no stopping once they began to cross the alkali desert. He also told them to make sure all of their oxen had good shoes on their hooves.

Once they reached the flatlands, they found what little grass was growing there had dried out, and the only other things growing nearby were numerous clumps of sagebrush. The trail led toward some high mountains in the distance and the men grumbled, concerned that they might have to cross them.

McCleary said, "Those are the Ruby Mountains, and we don't have to cross them. The trail leads to a valley at the base of the mountains where we will find water and grass. After that, the trail heads west and skirts around the north side of the Rubies. Before we reach the Humboldt, we will have to cross some more low mountains, and then, a long stretch of flatlands."

The Ruby Mountains, Nevada

On Towards the Humboldt River

McCleary told the group that they were two days away from the Humboldt River, their next water source. "You will be using all of the water in your barrels for yourselves and also the animals, but you can replenish that supply once we reach the river. After that, we will reach a place where the river sinks into the sands of a desert that will take us at least three nights and two days to cross. Because most of the water we will find out there will be poisoned by alkali, we will have to cross that stretch of desert without stopping. All of our water barrels will be emptied by the time we get across, and most of you will find you will have to abandon most of your heaviest belongings in the desert in order to keep your oxen alive!"

After he learned that the desert crossing would take all of two days and three nights, Tom struggled to put it out of his mind, but he'd had little success in doing so. Now, that was all he could think about. Martha's mother was not doing well. Her supply of patent medicine was exhausted, and her hacking cough kept her awake most of the night. Tom thought the old woman might have contracted tuberculosis and might not survive the journey, but he had not shared this with Martha. They would know soon enough.

The Humboldt River, NW Nevada

As predicted, it took two days to reach the Humboldt. The area around the riverbanks was covered with lush grass, and the animals feasted. It was decided that they would rest here for two days in order to ready the oxen, as well as the people, for the ordeal ahead. Everyone was well aware that a crossing that took three nights and two days would be punishing for all.

The river water tasted fresh, and everyone refilled the water barrels that had been emptied over the last two days. Of course, they would all drink from the river until they reached the desert, where they would start that dreaded crossing with full water barrels onboard. Mcleary advised everyone to find a small river rock that had been smoothed down by the running water and sand.

"If you wet it and place it in your mouth when you get dry, it will help you stay somewhat moist and reduce your craving for a drink."

The Humboldt Sink

When they reached the spot where the Humboldt sunk into the desert, they paused to rest the animals for that evening and all the following day. McCleary said they should start across the desert just after sunset the next day.

As soon as the wagons crossed onto the white-crusted alkali soil they all knew the crossing would be more difficult than they had imagined. It had rained some time before, and when the steel wagon tires broke through the crusted soil, they sunk into a sticky muck that clung to the wheel spokes, the feet of the oxen and also to everyone's shoes and boots. As each wagon passed, the ruts grew deeper. By the time Tom and Martha's wagon reached the start of the desert, the ruts were almost ten inches in depth. Their team of six oxen had to struggle hard to free the wheels and keep their wagon moving.

As the sun rose higher in the sky, the glare of its rays on the white soil was brutal. Also, where the alkali soil was dry, white dust coated everything, and it was extremely irritating to their eyes, noses and throats. Martha's mother started coughing and could not stop. Before long, everyone's lips began to crack, and some folks broke out their lard to coat them.

It was almost noon when the first water barrels were opened. McCleary advised them that no one should drink more than a quarter cup of water. "The oxen will need it more than you, because it is the animals who are working hardest to pull these heavy wagons. Also, everyone should start lightening their wagons and jettison everything here, except for food and water, in order to lighten the oxen's burden."

All the next morning, they saw the many objects others had discarded alongside the trail. There were beds, chests of drawers, rocking chairs, tables, chairs, and even a small piano that someone would surely miss playing when they reached California.

Martha's mother coughed nearly all of that day and into the night. When they woke up the next morning, they discovered the old woman had expired some time in her sleep. After her burial alongside the trail, there was a brief service held before the wagon train rolled on. Before they continued, Tom threw out the bed and cabinet he had made for the lady. Many of the other folks had already thrown out all of their furniture.

The next day, their supplies of water were almost exhausted after they had watered the animals. Many had started sucking on the small river rock that McCleary had advised them they should use, after wetting them with water remaining in the bottom of the barrels. That night the lack of sleep began to take its toll on all. The animals bawled in protest and had to be whipped to keep them from lying down. The men and animals were all exhausted but had to somehow keep moving or collapse.

Around dawn, at the end of the second night, the oxen started bawling and straining in their traces. The cattle and horses also started to run forward, and the men had an extremely difficult time restraining them. McCleary told them "Those animals smell water ahead. Unhitch your oxen teams from the wagons, but keep them yoked together. We can leave the wagons right here and bring the animals back after they have had their drink."

The water source proved to be a small spring. It was not tainted with alkali, but it was not large enough to permit refilling the water barrels. McCleary said the Truckee River was another day's drive ahead of them and that would provide enough water and grass to refresh the animals and refill the barrels. About ten miles past the Truckee River, they would head toward the southwest toward the Carson River, where they could stop and rest themselves and their animals for the final climb over the Carson Pass.

That night, while they were camped along the banks of the Truckee River, there was quite a disturbance among the animals. A number of men rushed out with their weapons, but when they reached the place where the animals had been grazing, they found that quite a few cattle had been driven off and were nowhere in sight. The men vowed to follow the tracks in the morning, but McCleary vetoed the idea.

He warned, "Those cattle were likely driven off by members of the Paiute tribe, and probably slaughtered and eaten by the tribe last night. You may find only bones and not many of those. The Paiutes are a sad lot, and will eat the entire animal, including the intestines and bone marrow. Folks have taken to calling them digger Indians because the tribe is usually seen digging up roots of wildflowers and cattails. Most of their meat comes from small animals such as ground squirrels and raccoons. A cow provides the whole tribe with a real feast that is quickly devoured. If you try chasing ghosts, you are likely to be left behind because we head out tomorrow morning for the Truckee River."

Paiute tribe members

It turned out that the Paiutes did not have to be hunted because they all appeared the next morning and started shooting at some of the cattle with their bows and arrows. They wounded several cows, and the men were quick to return fire and drove off the attackers. Most of the animals had mortal wounds and had to be put down. Their carcasses were left behind in hopes that this would satisfy the Paiutes if they returned after the train headed south. This tactic appeared to have worked because no other Paiutes were seen that day. However, McCleary said the tribe would probably try to drive off some more cattle that night and they would need to be closely guarded to prevent that.

Those who owned cattle agreed that they would stand guard that night, as long as they were in the Paiute territory. McCleary told them the raids would probably end when they reached Carson Pass. That was the edge of the territory claimed by the Washoe Tribe.

A Tense Night

The men guarded the cattle and horses closely that night, in order to prevent the loss of any more of their livestock. They were aware of the presence of some Paiutes who were using yips like a coyote and bird calls to communicate. Scattered clouds drifted past a half moon, cutting off the light. This gave the Paiutes a brief opportunity to creep toward the herd of animals in an attempt to drive a few off. When this happened, the men fired shots at sounds in the sagebrush, but they were firing blind and ending up wounding one cow that had to be put down with a shot to the head.

It was decided that the only way to ward off further attempts to drive off any more animals would be to have more of the men mount horses and continually circle the herd. Of course, the herd had already been spooked by the shots and they were constantly milling around and attempting to run off, which made it hard to maintain order. It proved to be a long, hard night.

The weather had started to change and the night was cold, and a chilly rain started to fall just around dawn. It was already the tenth of October and everyone was worried about the possibility of snow on top of the mountain pass. McCleary told them it was far too early for any heavy snowfall. He said they should not stop for any more rests before they reached the Truckee River, where they would turn to the southwest toward the Carson River. They started packing and hitching up the oxen without bothering to cook any breakfast the next morning.

As they started toward the west, the rain turned to sleet. They feared they would not see the sun that day, and in spite of what McCleary had said, some thought there might be snow on the ground the next morning. Everyone felt the chill that signaled the arrival of fall. That afternoon, they spied some Paiutes following them, just out of rifle shot range, and it was assumed they would probably have to guard against some more attempts at driving off livestock that night. They were right.

The riders circling the animals later that night came under attack and a number of arrows came flying at them from the darkness. Two men were hit, but only one of the wounds was serious. When they heard one of the wounded men cry for help, most of the men inside the wagon circle grabbed their rifles and rushed out to the herd to help drive off the attackers. The dark forms of the Paiutes presented targets, and several of them were wounded and one was slain. The natives finally scattered in all directions. McCleary said they might have seen the last of the Paiutes. He thought they would have been discouraged by the ferocity of the rifle fire and would probably be very hesitant to expose themselves to that threat again.

Headed for the Truckee River

Unfortunately, the ground was still wet when the train set out in a westerly direction for the Truckee River. The going was slow because the last stretch of the desert, near the banks of what appeared to be a huge lake of alkali water, had been soaked by the previous day's rain. The oxen hooves sunk into the muck with each step, and the wagon wheels cut ruts that were at least six inches deep. By the time Tom and Martha's wagon reached the edge of the lake, the ruts were almost a foot deep and their oxen team had to struggle to keep the wagon going, Martha remarked that it was fortunate that Tom had invested in a team of six oxen, rather than four.

The deep, muddy soil slowed their progress so much that it took a full day to reach the Truckee River. That river flowed in an easterly direction from an outlet on the northwest shore of Lake Tahoe, which was situated situated midway between the Donner and Carson Passes (as they are called today). At the place the wagon train reached the Truckee River, it had turned to the North where it emptied into the brackish Pyramid Lake. The water barrels all needed to be refilled and the men undertook this task while the women cooked a good dinner. They planned to head southwest toward the Carson River quite early the next morning, so the women made cornbread, wrapped it up in cloth and put it away for a hasty breakfast.

It was October 11th, and a cold wind was blowing when they awoke before dawn and prepared to depart their camp near the east bank of the Truckee. After they ate, the women packed and the men gathered their oxen, yoked them up and hitched the teams to the wagons. They had a long day's drive ahead of them before they would reach the Carson River.

By now, all of the members of the train had chapped skin and lips. Many had applied a coating of lard to prevent their lips from cracking. Everyone had hoped for an Indian Summer, the warm spell in early Fall when the Indian women were all out harvesting the seeds they would use that Winter to make flour for preparing their fry bread. It now seemed that this year there might not be an Indian Summer after all, and they might start to see the snow fly before long.

Bad weather did not take long to arrive. The cold wind blew from the north instead of from the west, as it normally did in this region of the country. Before long, the wind was accompanied by a driving sleet. Fortunately, the wagon train was headed in a southwesterly direction, so the wind and sleet were coming at their backs, instead of right in their faces. Still, all were feeling the harsh effects of the abrupt change of weather. Regardless of their present discomfort, the major concern was whether or not there would be a large accumulation of snow when they crossed Carson Pass. The tragic plight of the Donner Party was on everyone's mind, even though McCleary continued to assure them that they would be able to get across the pass before a great amount of snow could trap them as it had the Donner Party on October 30th.

Reaching the Carson River

After a long and uncomfortable day, they reached the Carson River. There was a large grove of Cottonwood trees growing near the north bank of the river and a thick patch of willows on the south. A handful of Paiute women were gathering long, green willow branches and were stripping them of their leaves and twigs. The women quickly departed as soon as the

Carson River, Nevada

wagon train arrived. Just before dark, three of the women, accompanied by three Paiute men, came walking back to the circle of wagons. The women were carrying some woven baskets they had woven from willow branches. Some of those branches had been stained red, light brown and black and woven in a way that the baskets were decorated in beautiful patterns.

The native women signed that they wished to trade the baskets for food, and the pioneer women were more than willing to do so. Soon some of the casks of remaining meat were opened and portions of salt pork were being portioned out for trade. Martha had thought to bring along a large supply of sugar for Tom's coffee, and she decided to offer a little of it to trade for a particularly beautiful basket. The basket maker did not know what sugar was and thought she was being offered salt. It seemed she was eager to trade, but when she took a taste of the sweet granules, her eyes flew open in surprise, and she would have none of it. The sugar was taken back and an equal amount of salt was offered, which she readily accepted in trade for her basket.

Then Martha gave the woman's child a small taste of sugar, and the young girl signed that she would like more. Martha gave her a small paper envelope that she had filled one-quarter full. The girl's mother seemed fascinated by the envelope, and Martha gave her a sheet of writing paper with some pretty colored Spring flowers printed at the top. The woman was thrilled, hugged Martha, and ran off to show the other two native women her prize. Martha quickly put away the paper because she had no intention of giving away any more of the special writing paper that she had brought to write letters to each of her friends in Spring-field once they reached California.

There was just one hill that stood between them and the rugged mountains in the distance. McCleary in-tended that they should camp in the valley that was only a day's ride from the base of those mountains the next evening. They would then reach the foot of Carson Pass the following day. It was just after sunset when the Paiutes departed, and several sentries were posted.

Not long after sunset, a shot rang out. McCleary had ridden out to hunt, and when he returned, he had a large deer carcass draped behind his saddle. The man who offered to dress and butcher it was quite amazed at the length of the deer's ears. McCleary told him that it was a mule deer, a species that was not found east of the Rocky Mountains. The backstraps were roasted and taken out to the sentries for their supper. The rest of the venison was used to make a stew.

The wind blew throughout the whole night but then died down just before dawn. Sunrise brought welcome warmth, and the sky was a brilliant blue and clear of any clouds. It appeared that at last they might have a most welcome Indian-Summer day. Everyone cooked and ate breakfast, and packed up, anxious to be on their way toward their last obstacle—the mountains ahead. Of course, as McCleary had pointed out, they were still two days away.

The trail following the river had only a few bends they called "oxbows." The hill was crossed without much difficulty, even though it was a long climb. It was apparent that the slow-moving oxen were tired, so it was decided to make an early camp alongside the river in the large valley ahead of them.

Some Paiute women approached the camp not long after the wagons were circled and offered a large basket of small, greenish nuts in trade for salt. The pioneers had never seen nuts like these. After tasting a few, they decided they were quite a treat. The pioneers were curious and wanted to know where the nuts grew. Following a short exchange of sign language, the Indians pointed toward some short pine trees growing on a range of hills in the distance to the North. The pioneers decided to call them the Pine Nut Hills.*

*The Pine Nut Hills are technically part of what geologists named the Virginia Range, but even today, locals refer to them as The Pine Nuts.)

An hour before sunrise the next morning, they set out heading for the mountains that loomed in the distance. Since they had stopped early the night before, they would have a longer ride that day. McCleary told them the range of mountains ahead of them was not the Sierra Nevada Mountains. It had been named the Carson Range after the explorer Kit Carson.

The Sierra Nevada Mountains rose just beyond them, and would be reached just after they had topped the ridge and camped that night in a lovely high meadow where they were able to catch some cutthroat trout to fry for their breakfast the following morning.

McCleary explained that these are called "cutthroats" because they have a bright, orange-red stripe behind their chin. Early pioneers called them salmon trout. In fact, the Truckee River, that they had left two days ago, was originally named the Salmon Trout River. It was later renamed the Truckee River after Chief Truckee, the leader of the Washoe tribe.

As they ate the trout, McCleary told the pioneers about the Washoe tribe that spends much of the year camped around Lake Tahoe, located about fifteen miles north of there.

"They catch and smoke trout, which they can eat in the Winter after they migrate down to the Carson Valley. I can still recall the good smoky taste of the trout that some members of the Washoe tribe once gave me."

McCleary continued reminiscing, "You know, this valley may be the only territory in the country that three Indian tribes share without conflict. The Washoe go down to collect pine nuts in the fall, as do the Paiutes, and the Shoshones ride their spotted horses down from the North to spend the Winter in the sunny valley and marshes that are created when the Truckee River floods after the Spring thaw. All three tribes hunt the ducks and geese that stop there on their flights southward from Canada."

He continued, "Even though those tribes are said to winter there every year without any conflict, there is an old tale about the Paiutes and Shoshone fighting a war, and the terms of the peace was that the Paiutes were to never own or ride horses. However, I have serious doubts that the Paiutes ever owned any horses in the first place. I have yet to see a mounted Paiute, and I suspect that they will eat any stray horses they manage to catch!"

When they awoke, there was a strong wind blowing from the west. It was a warm wind but stronger than the one that had blown down from the north as they left the Truckee River. When Tom commented on how the wind direction, speed and temperature changed in this region of the country, McCleary said, "This wind originated somewhere out in the Pacific Ocean, maybe even as far away as the Cook Islands. The cold wind the other day probably blew down all the way from Russia, passing over Alaska and British Columbia and the Oregon Territory. Now I've been told by folks who Wintered over in this area that winds in the Spring, called Chinooks, will blow down into this valley from the tops of the Sierras and can reach hurricane speeds."

Tom was not sure what hurricane speeds were, but he had experienced tornado winds in Illinois and he imagined them to be something like that.

McCleary continued, "Chinooks are the names for the winds that blow down in the spring from the glaciers toward the valleys that are warming below. They have them in Alaska and in Sweden and Norway, where they are called *foehns,* or some such thing."

Tom was impressed with all of the knowledge McCleary had regarding geography and climatic conditions, and he asked him where he had learned so much.

"Well, I signed up as a lad, on a whaling ship out of New England, not long after arriving here from Scotland. We sailed all the way to Finland and Portugal and then back across the Atlantic, sailed around Cape Horn and out to the Cook Islands. Now those were some extremely strong and cold winds you have to fight coming around the horn. We beat against them for five days before the Captain decided that, since they couldn't make way sailing west against them, he would sail south to get around them!"

He continued, "We sailed for days to the southwest. We sailed so long that we encountered icebergs, turned west and sailed almost to New Zealand and then back to the Cook Islands in pursuit of those damned whales. As a lad I learned things from sailors who had come from many places, like Jamaica and Samoa, and among them there were some men who had sailed past both Cape Horn and the Cape of Good Hope around South Africa. Sailors talk about sailing the Seven Seas, but they've told me that those are only the seven around the British Isles and Europe. I know there are many more seas than seven to sail in this world, but most I can't name."

They traveled all day and reached a place where the Carson River tumbled down a narrow cut in the mountains to their base.

McCleary told them, "You can plan to rest your oxen a day at the flats above the last waterfall and allow them to feed for a day before starting up the steep and rocky grade. There will be little feed for them in the mountains."

Everyone enjoyed the rest and an opportunity to bathe in the Carson River's waters. The women found a pool with cattails and pounded their roots to make a kind of soap that they used to wash their hair.

Later, some of the men and boys fished for trout and were able to catch enough for all to have for breakfast together with their fried bread. Because some of the ladies had no flour left, it was decided to pool all that was left in the train and divide it so that every family could have some *johnny cakes*. It would be the last they would have on the journey.

From now it would have to be fried cornbread until they reached Sacramento and purchased some supplies for the Winter. Tom had no funds left, so he and Martha would have to rely on his brother in Coloma to get them through that first Winter. After that, he could start making and selling furniture.

Up the Carson River Canyon

After the day of rest, the train started their way up the trail over the mountains ahead. The first mile was not too difficult, but the grade was steeper beyond that and it was also littered with large boulders that had washed down the steep sides of the mountain on their right. Many of the smaller, loose rocks had been swept down the hill and onto the trail by past landslides, but there were many larger ones stuck in the ground that the wagons had to lurch over. There were several wagon wheels broken on these rocks. Also, a lot of wagons had started to come apart in various places as a result of the many miles of rough ground they had traversed. Tom and Martha's wagon was in surprisingly good shape. The wagons built by the Studebaker Brothers were constructed with the best kiln-dried oak available and handcrafted with the utmost care.

After struggling many hours to get the wagons over only three miles of the steep and rocky trail, both the oxen and men were exhausted. There were small ponds in the flat canyon. Some of the young lads ran ahead and came back exclaiming that the ponds contained cutthroat trout. Everyone was pleased to think they would have another breakfast of fried trout coated with cornmeal, and the boys were sent back to hastily cut some willow fishing poles and split open several rotten logs to find grubs for bait. The men planned to join them as soon as the oxen were unyoked.

McCleary said this would be the best place for their last rest to allow the oxen to regain their strength for the hard climb over the Sierras. He said it would take at least three days to cross over and begin the downhill trek to the Sacramento Valley. This meant another trout breakfast, something everyone relished. Tom missed having some eggs for breakfast. The hens had not survived the forty-mile desert crossing and had been boiled for a chicken stew several days ago, when the wagon train reached the Truckee River.

Three men, who were traveling on horseback with the train and had a pack of mules loaded with goods, decided they would ride north to find Lake Tahoe and trade with the Washoe tribe, who were said to be peaceful. They said they planned to cross the Sierras and travel to Sacramento, following the same route as the Donner Party. Of course, no one else decided to join them with their wagons, and not one of them would ever see the deep blue lake that was twelve miles wide and twenty miles long and filled with crystal clear water.

Martha had not had time to make any pea soup so far on the journey, so that evening she got out her entire supply of dried peas. Some of the other families added theirs, and together there was enough to start several pots of soup. She got out the last of their salt pork, cut it into small chunks and divided the pieces to add to each pot for flavor. The other women who were cooking with her remarked how kind she was to share her food with everyone. She replied, "I believe we should share our blessings, as well as the travails on this journey west. The hardest part appears to be ahead of us, so we should enjoy this respite before undertaking the final climb."

After their day of rest and another trout breakfast, the pioneers started on a trail that gradually sloped toward the west. One of their party exclaimed, "This is an easy climb. If it continues like this, we will be over in no time."

After they topped the slope, the trail wound around a large, high mountain lake that had a thin coating of ice. The nights at these elevations were brutally cold, even though the men and animals sweated in the daytime sun. After a steep run downhill, where they had to place branches in the wagon spokes to help slow the descent of the wagons, the trail rose sharply toward some huge granite outcroppings.

Far below the granite cliffs on their left lay another deep-blue lake surrounded by a granite shoreline. McCleary told them that he had explored this lake, swam in it, and dove down to the bottom to discover it was essentially a huge granite bowl. He added that it was the coldest water he had ever ventured into.

"Why, it must be one-hundred-percent snow melt. You might not be bathing in that water, I guess," he added with a chuckle.

After a two-mile downgrade that was easily traversed, the trail rose sharply ahead of them. At the top they found a wooden sign that had the words TRAGEDY SPRINGS carved on it. Everyone wondered what the tragedy was. Even McCleary was not aware of what it was, but he said "There are no lack of tragedies on this trail. Lord knows what this one was!" The sign stirred grim thoughts among the group, and they were glad to move on a few more miles.

The next time they hit a flat area, they wanted to stop for the night, but McCleary said they needed to keep traveling as far as they could that day because of some signs of a change in the weather.

"There are dark clouds on the horizon, and if a storm hits here there will no doubt be some snow on the ground tomorrow morn. If there is, we need to be closer to the tops of these mountains, if not on the top. Going downhill through snow will be far easier than going up, as the Donner party found out." He continued, "In fact, it proved fatal for many of them!"

The Sierra Nevada Mountains

Everyone agreed to push on and get to the top of the mountains that night, even if it meant rolling on after sunset. They continued on their way by the light of a full moon. After reaching the highest point on the trail, everyone skipped dinner and turned in quite early, because they were all anxious to start their way downhill toward Sacramento the next morning.

Down the Sierras Toward Their Destination

McCleary's voice could be heard through the camp before dawn, shouting, "We have a foot of snow on the ground and it is still coming down. There is no time for a fire and cooking breakfast. We need to be on our way now!" This greatly troubled Martha because a letter she had received from Margret Reed last year described how they had been trapped by an early snowstorm close to the top of the pass.

Martha asked McCleary if they were facing a similar situation, and he replied, "Not at all. The Donner Party still had to try to make their way up an extremely steep grade to reach the top of the pass, and we have already reached it. We will be able to make our way through a foot of snow fairly easily, but we need to get going, since it is still piling up. Now, please get yourself ready to go!"

The previous morning, Martha had used the last of their cornmeal to fry a large batch of hush puppies that she had packed away. She unpacked these and after setting aside a few for Tom, James and herself, she went around and gave each of the children pieces of the cakes. When she got back to their wagon, James and Tom had packed everything and hitched up the team of oxen and saddled their mules.

When the train started the downhill grade through the foot of snow, Tom realized there was at least one benefit to being the last wagon in line. The wagon wheels and oxen had packed down the snow on the trail. However, the extreme cold started freezing the wet snow and the oxen were slipping as they pulled the wagon downhill. Tom hoped that none of the oxen would break an ankle or a leg as a result of slipping on the ice.

The snowfall continued all day, and McCleary told everyone that they could stop at noon, cook some soup for their only meal of the day, and continue to make their way downhill past sunset. They could travel by the light of the full moon because the clouds were now passing to the East. Everyone agreed this would be the wisest thing to do—considering the weather.

Tom's fear about an injury to one of his oxen was not unwarranted. One of his lead oxen slipped on the ice and broke an ankle, laming it, and he had to put it down. He learned that another team of four oxen had been reduced to three, so he offered one of his to take its place. His team of four remaining oxen should have no problem pulling their wagon on the downhill trail toward the foothills above the Sacramento valley.

The oxen meat was cut into pieces for the soup they immediately started cooking for the train's only meal. Some folks contributed a few potatoes, a handful of withered carrots, and some dried onions for the stewpots, soon bubbling on a couple of large fires. The soup warmed everyone and even seemed to lift their spirits for the long, cold trek ahead. The snowfall continued until about an hour before sunset, when the clouds started breaking up. They were then treated to a colorful sunset with purple and pink clouds.

"When you finally reach California, you will witness many more multicolored sunsets such as this one as the sun sinks below the horizon over the Pacific Ocean. I myself have witnessed many such sunsets as we sailed west across that ocean on our hunt for whales. There was a saying we repeated so often that went: *Red skies at night, sailors delight. Red skies at morning, sailors take warning.* So, we may wake to a clear sky tomorrow."

McCleary's prediction proved to be true. They awoke to a clear sky and a quickly rising temperature, as the sun rose over the top of mountains behind them. In fact, it finally grew warm enough by noon that the two feet of snow started melting, and the trail became a mire of wet snow and mud. Now Tom's team of oxen had a harder task ahead of them, as there was one long upgrade before they started downhill again. Other teams started slipping and sliding as they labored uphill along the sloppy trail.

McCleary decided that since the snowstorm had let up, they could take the time to double-team the oxen to handle that final steep grade. Of course, this took a lot of extra time, and it was late in the afternoon before every wagon had made it to the top. Everyone wanted to stop for an early dinner, and McCleary decided both the pioneers and their animals needed a rest.

Everyone had used up their supply of meat and some of the men wanted to go hunting for deer or a bear, but McCleary told them all the deer had migrated to the foothills below the mountains for the Winter, and the bears were now hibernating in their dens. McCleary said finding a bear den would probably take them hours. In a day or two they should reach the foothills ahead and there should be deer in abundance that they could hunt and feast on.

The next day was much easier than the previous two with the lack of snow and the downhill terrain. However, when they reached the foothills it started to rain heavily, and soon low spots in the trail were filling with water. The trail itself had turned to mud, and all the wagon drivers were having a hard time keeping their oxen moving because their hooves were sinking in the deep muck.

The men who were anxious to go hunt deer hunting said that there was little chance of finding any out in such a heavy rain. Deer usually bed down under some protective trees during this kind of storm. They said there might be a chance of spotting one bedded down under the oak trees growing in the foothills. They were perplexed because these oaks still had green leaves, which was strange for this late in the year.

McCleary told them "Those are live oaks. They shed some of their leaves all year, and the leaves left on the trees stay green all year. You will also find that the grass starts growing this time of year in California, stays green all Winter and dries out around June, when the rains stop for the Summer. The rains don't fall again until October. This is just the opposite of what you are used to seeing in the Midwest."

They saw no deer bedded-down beneath the oaks and one hunter exclaimed, "They are being spooked by the noise of the wagon train. If a few of us ride a quarter of a mile or so, we might have a better chance of finding a deer or two."

Five men with rifles rode ahead, and about a half hour later, a volley of shots was heard. When the train had reached the hunters, McCleary saw they had killed four elk. The animals were not much larger than the mule deer they had shot earlier and they had light tan-colored coats and white hair on their shoulders and heads.

McCleary told them, "Those are called Tule Elk. They are smaller and lighter colored than the larger elk found around the Rocky Mountains. Still, these four will provide a good supper for everyone."

Early the next morning the hunters took their shotguns and killed ten geese at some nearby ponds. Since the pioneer's food supplies were exhausted, any kind of wild game the hunters were able to harvest was a welcome bounty. McCleary said that the folks who had brought enough hard cash should be able to purchase enough food for the Winter at Sutter's Fort. Those with little or no funds could probably sell off some of their livestock and possibly their wagons, provided they were in fair shape. Tom told Martha they should be able to sell all of their oxen as well as their fine wagon, which had held up quite well. However, he had grown quite fond of his Hawken rifle and decided he would keep it if he could.

Sacramento at Last!

When they finally reached Sacramento, McCleary told everyone that those pioneers who wanted to raise grain or cattle should travel North, and those who wanted to grow other crops should head South. Tom asked directions to his brother's sawmill in Coloma and was informed that, after discovering gold, James Marshall had purchased a large house built in the heart of Sacramento. When they arrived and were warmly greeted by James and his wife, they were told they were welcome to stay until Tom was able to buy or build a house for himself and Martha. So, at last, the long and arduous journey to California was over.

This was the place they dreamed of coming to when they left Springfield almost seven months ago. Their handsome young teamster, James Wilson, proposed marriage to the pretty Irish lass. They were married and raised four children, all of which had red hair and freckled faces.

5 ❖ The Buffalo Hunters

The first white men who came to the Great Plains to hunt buffalo used muzzle-loading rifles. At first, there were few hunters, and their hunts were usually tolerated by some of the tribes. However, neither the Blackfeet nor the Pawnee had tolerance for anyone hunting within what they considered their hunting territories, especially white men. Often any of the trespassers who were unlucky enough to be captured suffered a sad, brutal ending, often involving torture.

By the late 1800s, breech-loading single-shot rifles chambered for large caliber ammunition had been developed. The favorite of many buffalo hunters was the Sharps 45–90, which fired a .45 caliber lead bullet loaded in a brass cartridge case packed with 90 grains of black powder. Also popular was the Remington Rolling Block rifle that was available in a choice of either 45–70, 45–90, or 50–100 calibers. Both the Sharps and Remington rifles proved to be extremely effective at a distance of up to five hundred yards.

Then, white hunters, who were equipped with those long-range rifles, began what was called "market hunting." Buffalo skins were made into coats and blankets for the extremely cold Winter climate at the time. Vast quantities of the beasts were shot and skinned merely for their hides and tongues The latter were "pickled" by being packed in brine in wooden barrels. Two of the hunters who earned their reputation by killing numerous buffalo were Kit Carson (cited as the greatest of all of the hunters) and William "Buffalo Bill" Cody.

The number of buffalo slaughtered was enormous. Between 1872 and 1874, the railroads hauled 1,379,000 buffalo hides East, and after the hunting had ended, 32,000,000 pounds of bones were gathered from the plains to be ground into fertilizer. It's been estimated that 4,500,000 buffalo were killed just in the region adjacent to the west of the Arkansas River.

The slaughter of the buffalo herds by the whites was a sad page in the history of the west. Besides almost eliminating the American Bison species, it also caused the certain and swift elimination of the horse culture of the Natives of the West. Some claim this actually may have been the intention of the Market Hunters. However, it is more likely that it was just plain greed on their part once they had decided to make their living hunting buffalo.

Pile of buffalo skulls (1892)

The first buffalo hunters in the tall-grass prairies of the American West were tribes of Natives, who hunted by following the huge herds that migrated between the Rocky Mountains and the Mississippi River. There was such a large population of buffalo that tribes, such as the Arapahoe, Blackfeet, Cheyenne, Crow, Kaw, Kiowas, Pawnee, Shoshone, and Sioux, subsisted primarily by hunting only that species.

Before the Spaniards reintroduced the horse to North America, two hundred years after they became extinct there, the Natives had two methods of hunting buffalo. A single hunter would put the head and skin of a buffalo calf over his back and crawl on all fours toward the herd, pretending to be an orphaned calf. He'd drag a spear tied to a strip of hide to his leg, and when close enough to a lone animal he'd spear it. Then, if the herd stampeded, only a single buffalo might be harvested.

A more effective way to harvest buffalo was to line a whole tribe up near a herd and stampede it toward a cliff or steep bluff. After many of the animals that made the jump were crippled with broken legs, necks or backs, they could be easily killed with a lance or knife.

The third method came after the tribes finally acquired herds of wild horses. Mounted hunters would ride alongside the fleeing buffalo herd using their bow and arrows. Then the women, who followed behind the mounted hunters on foot, would butcher the animals. The meat would be loaded on travois, which were dragged back to their camps. Whatever meat was not consumed at a feast that night would be smoked and stored for food in the Winter. Dried buffalo meat was primarily what the tribes subsisted on after the herds migrated South from their Summer grazing lands.

The Decision

Eric Strawn had a decision to make. His best friend Ralph Turner wanted him to join him on a long journey into the wilds of the West to hunt buffalo. Most of the herds in the area to the west of the Arkansas river had been hunted out, and Ralph wanted the two of them to leave Fort Smith, Arkansas and travel West to the territory of Wyoming. Eric was not sure he wanted to venture out into country he had no knowledge of. Also, he had never shot anything larger than a razorback hog with a low-powered .44 caliber Henry Rifle he'd once borrowed from his uncle.

"There is a fortune to be made in buffalo skins,

and I hear the land out west is teeming with herds of the beasts," Ralph had declared. Ralph was the best hunter and fisherman Eric knew, but he was very impulsive and always seeking adventure. Eric was just the opposite, and it was very strange that the two were friends. Ralph always wanted to push the limits of propriety. In fact, he had a bad reputation. One man said that Ralph Turner would shoot your milk cow and claim he thought it was a deer, if he thought he could get to keep some of the meat.

Although you never knew what trouble he was going to get you into, it was nevertheless exciting to pair up with Ralph. As boys, the two of them would quite often steal fruit from many of their neighbor's fruit trees or from watermelon patches. One night, Ralph had silently crept into the unlocked back door of a house, while the folks inside were sleeping, and made off with a large sum of cash that the lady of the house kept in her cookie jar. When he got older, Ralph used to like to drink a lot and have his way with loose women; whereas, Eric didn't have a taste for liquor and actually had no experience with ladies of any sort because he was shy.

Eric argued, "We don't have the provisions or rifles to set off for Wyoming to hunt buffalo."

Ralph countered, "I can break into Wilson's Hardware. I heard they just got in a case of 45–90 Remington Rolling Block rifles. That is the best caliber because they'll shoot a lot further than a 45–70 and are more accurate than a 50–100. He's got all the gear we'll need, and we can load up one of my uncle's covered freight wagons and be off before daybreak."

Ralph convinced Eric that they could get away with this larceny because he'd learned the Sheriff was out of town for a week, and they could not be easily tracked once their wagon tracks were mingled with all of the others on the road to Dodge City, Kansas. Eric grew excited with the prospect of seeing the west, and in a moment of weakness, he agreed he'd go with Ralph, as long as he was not the one who had to steal the rifles and all of the provisions they needed.

On Their Way

Before sunrise the next morning, they were well on their way to Dodge City. Eric had packed up all the food he had in the house and he'd pocketed his modest life savings to boot. They were on their way to Wyoming to hunt bufallo! Later that day, they decided they were not being pursued. The two planned to follow the Arkansas River from Kansas into Colorado and then head North along the east side of the Rocky Mountains until they reached Wyoming

During their long journey, Ralph did a fair job of keeping them supplied with fresh meat, because he was quite an excellent shot with his new Remington. Because he'd had little experience shooting, Eric was just a fair shot with his. However, Ralph's skill with the stolen rifle more than made up for that. He told Eric that he should at least be able to hit something as large as a buffalo.

Their trip was not uneventful. One night, several young Kaw braves tried to steal some of the provisions from the wagon, but they knocked over a cast-iron Dutch oven that made enough noise to wake Ralph, and he sprang from the bed he'd made on the ground. He yelled at the would-be thieves as he picked up his loaded rifle that was always beside him at night.

"You injuns come back again, and I'll send the both of you to the happy huntin' grounds!" Following that oath, the prairie echoed with the boom of his 45–90, as the lead bullet he'd fired zipped between the two Kaw's heads.

The two men had seen members of other tribes as they traveled toward Wyoming Territory, but they never bothered them. That was probably because they had not been shooting buffalo, the primary source of food for those tribes. Of course, as long as the white hunters only killed one, or two at the most, it was of no consequence. If they took more than what could be eaten by them, the Whites might have a battle on their hands!

A Sad Sight

When Eric and Ralph finally reached Wyoming Territory, they found evidence of what the "market hunters" had done that triggered the anger of the tribes so greatly. The two topped a bluff, and lying on the expanse of grassland before them were the rotting carcasses of hundreds of buffalo. They had been stripped of their hides, as well as their tongues. Later that day, they saw the smoke from a prairie fire ahead. There was a wind coming from the Southwest that was driving the fire to the Northeast, away from them.

After traveling about a mile, they saw where the fire had been started. Two fully loaded wagons were in the process of burning to the ground. Eric had no idea of just how sickening the scene would be. When they reached the wagons, Eric was shocked to see there were four bodies lying on the ground!

The wagon to the rear had been loaded with wooden barrels filled with pickled buffalo tongues. Most of the barrels were just charred because they were filled with brine. However, one had been hacked open and turned on its side, and a number of tongues had been pulled out. Apparently, these had been consumed or taken for a future meal by the attacking savages.

The other wagon was stacked with wet buffalo hides and the stench of their burning fat and hair was stomach-turning. However, the sight of the four naked bodies of the market hunters lying nearby was the worst sight Eric had ever seen. Each of the bodies had been shot with numerous arrows, mutilated, and their scalps taken. All of the dead hunters had their eyes poked out. Ralph told Eric that this was often done because some Natives believed that without eyes, a dead soul was doomed to wander the Earth and never make their way to their final resting place, or what the Natives called the "Happy Hunting Ground."

The End of the Journey

Eric at once declared, "I am going no further. I am not willing to risk my life to hunt buffalo and end up lying on the ground like these poor souls! If you are not willing to turn this wagon around right now and head back to civilization, then I will walk back!"

Ralph said he had lost interest in the buffalo hunting as well, and would head the wagon East. He decided he would rather try his luck at becoming a gambler. Eric said he wanted to head for Iowa. He had heard that the Union Pacific Railroad was hiring men at Council Bluffs to help them build a railroad across the United States, and he intended to take part in this exciting endeavor.

Ralph was shot and killed sometime after he'd started his chosen occupation after being caught cheating at poker in Dodge City.

Golden Spike Ceremony at Promontory Point, Utah

The Union Pacific Railroad hired Eric as a pay-master. After the Union Pacific had joined their line with the Central Pacific at Promontory Point, Utah, he traveled west to Sacramento and ended up working as a clerk for the Crocker Bank, and later became the banks' manager. He met a pretty young Swedish girl whose family had come to California on the first west-bound train from Chicago, Illinois. They were married, and raised a son and three daughters in the booming town of Sacramento.

6 ❖ The Chinaman

Starting Out

His name was Chu Han, and he was born in 1835 in a small village near the outskirts of Shanghai. His father was a tailor and his mother sold the clothing his father made at a stall she owned at a market near the outskirts of the city. As a young child, Chu was cared for by his grandmother who died when he was fourteen years old. From then on—he cared for himself.

Chu did not look like the typical Chinese male. His skin was much lighter colored, and his hair was somewhat curly. This was because his mother was Eurasian, the result of a tender, but very brief, union between his quite attractive grandmother and a Portuguese sailor. He was a junior officer on one of the "black sailing ships" used for trade between the Mediterranean Ocean and the South China Sea.

Missionaries had converted his father many years ago from Buddhism to Catholicism. He decided that Chu should be educated in the mission school. Therefore, Chu was not only well educated, but he also spoke fluent English. His father attempted to interest him in becoming a tailor when he was finished with his schooling, but he had no interest in the trade.

A Chance to Become a Seaman

Some of the older boys he knew had decided to become crewmen on Chinese trading vessels, called "junks," which sailed out of Shanghai carrying goods to other ports along the coast of China. Some of the traders had even sailed to ports on the other side of the South China Sea. The idea of a sailor's life fascinated him, so Chu asked one of his friends if he would help him find employment as a seaman's apprentice on the vessel his friend served on. Chu was hired and believed that before long he would become a seasoned crewman on an ocean-going sailing vessel. He might have become what he hoped to be, but during his maiden voyage, the vessel was damaged by a typhoon and was put into dry dock for an extensive rebuilding. Chu was already out of his first job at the age of sixteen.

Chu was hanging around the docks one afternoon when he saw a young man being carried off an American sailing vessel on a litter heading for the hospital. When the litter bearers returned with the empty litter, Chu asked the men about the sick sailor they had just carried off. He was informed that he was their cabin boy who was suffering from a case of dysentery and could not sail with them that evening on the turn of the tide. Chu asked if he could come aboard and apply for the job, and after the crewman discussed this with the ship's First Mate, he was told that he was more than welcome to do so.

The First Mate who interviewed him told Chu to get his seabag and return to the ship as soon as he could or forget the job. He said they could always hire the next young man they found on the dock. Chu was back and on board in less than an hour. He was ready to become a member of the crew of a sailing ship—hopefully one bound for America!

American Clipper Ship

She was a fine vessel, built skillfully of native oak from the east coast of America. She'd been sailed through the same typhoon that had damaged Chu's last sea-going home, but had suffered nothing more than a broken spar and a tattered foresail. Chu learned that his duties were to care for the Captain's cabin and also the quarters occupied by the ship's Sailing Master and First Mate. Those quarters were to be kept spotless at all times, and he was expected to wash their clothes, as well as assist the ship's cook with his duties. This included helping with both the preparation and serving of food, and washing dishes. This was hardly the exciting sailor's life Chu had been looking forward to, and he decided to do what some of the sailors referred to as "jumping ship" when they reached the first port in America.

Many Chinese had told Chu that there was gold scattered on the ground at the base of the mountains in California. He believed that this may have been true because a man had returned to his village in China after making his fortune by pulling gold out of the earth in a place the Chinese called "Gum Shaw" (Gold Mountain). This place was supposedly located on the Western slopes of a great mountain range whose peaks were covered with ice and snow all year long.

Welcome Aboard!

When Chu was shown the crew's quarters and given the hammock formerly used by the previous cabin boy, he told the crew he would not use the hammock until it had been thoroughly washed. Most of the men were rude and told Chu that he was welcome to sleep on the deck for all they cared. However, one polite young seaman apprentice told Chu that he could tie a line to the hammock, then toss it overboard, and the action of the rushing salt water would clean it thoroughly. Chu thanked him profusely.

A New Name for Chu

The First Mate had told the crewmen Chu's name, and they all laughed and made fun of it. One crewman asked, "Are you going to chew our tough meat for us?" Another said "choo choo" were the words his son used when describing the steam engine for a train. Chu was embarrassed and told them that since he was going to become an American, he was going to adopt the name John. He was pleased with the way the two names John and Han rhymed, but did not care for the way John was spelled with an h. He was afraid some people would pronounce his name "Johan Han."

A Norwegian crewmember mentioned that in his country the name John was spelled Jan, but pronounced "Yahn." Chu said that he did not care for the sound of Yahn Han either, so he decided to spell his new first name Jon. He told the whole crew that he expected to be addressed as Jon from then on. Sensing that he was quite serious about his decision, and knowing he was the last person who would be handling their dishes before they ate from them, every one of his fellow crewmembers agreed that from that day forward, Chu would be Jon.

The Eastward voyage was tedious at times, as the ship sailed with a cargo of rice to Singapore, then transported hardwood from Singapore to Hawaii, then pineapple to Chile and finally, barrels of hard apple cider and red wine to San Francisco. After they sailed past what the sailors said was "the golden gate," Jon was astonished to see that the great bay was crowded with what looked like hundreds of abandoned ships whose crews had all jumped ship to become gold miners!

San Francisco Bay in 1850

Off the Ship and on to Chinatown

Jon went ashore while the crew was busy unloading the barrels and he walked uphill towards a place that one of the sailors had called "Chinatown." It was, as another crewman described, "full of Chinese people." When he arrived, Jon experienced a sharp pang of homesickness. This soon passed when he asked one of the residents for advice on how to get to Gold Mountain. He was told that if he wanted to mine gold, he should find his way Southeast to a place called "Chinese Camp," because the White miners in this country usually would not tolerate Chinese people mining alongside any of the claims they had staked out. When he asked for more detailed directions to Chinese Camp, Jon was advised to find an older Chinese man who had once mined gold, but now had opened a shop where he carved ivory and walrus tusks. It was located on what people called "Market Street," which he could find about a mile South of Chinatown.

San Francisco, 1851

The ivory carver's shop was not hard to find, and the elderly gentleman proved to be most willing to provide directions to Chinese Camp. He directed Jon to travel along the Western shoreline of San Francisco Bay until he reached the settlement of San Jose, where the

Spaniards had built a mission. The old man also said that, since Jon wore a crucifix, which the Missionaries had given him at his graduation, the good friars at Mission San Jose would likely provide him with some food and drink as well as a place to rest that night, if he asked them politely for assistance.

The carver also presented Jon with a woven willow basket that had two canvas straps attached to it, which could serve as a backpack. Inside the basket were some items Jon would need when he reached Chinese Camp. The carver said he had once used these items but no longer needed them. There was a short-handled spade, a gold pan, a fire-starting flint rock and steel, a skin water flask, and a steel pot for cooking. He also gave Jon a handful of rice cakes and a bag of dried seaweed to flavor any soup he decided to boil. Jon thanked the man and offered to pay for the items, but the offer was graciously declined.

On the Way to "Gold Mountain"

After the good friars provided their hospitality, Jon was told to head in an Eastward direction toward a canyon that wound through a high range of hills, then cross another, much higher hill and walk many miles toward the rising sun, until he reached a river. Following its Southern bank would lead him into the foothills of the high mountains. The friars told him that at this time of year swarms of large silver fish would be swimming up the river, and they could be easily speared or even caught by hand. Their tasty red flesh should provide all the food he needed for the journey.

Jon was advised that when he reached the mountains, there should be miners who could direct him to the place where the other Chinese men were mining. In fact, he might not even have to tell them he needed directions, since many of the White gold miners tended to dictate to the Chinese, in no uncertain terms, that they were not welcome to mine alongside them and often drove them South toward this "Chinese Camp." This, in fact, proved to be the case.

When Jon finally reached his destination, he found very few inhabitants there. He was told that all of the gold had been mined, and many of the Chinese miners had headed North to the settlement of Sacramento to seek work. Jon decided that employment there might provide him with a more reliable source of funds than trying to mine gold—something he knew absolutely nothing about.

Heading Back to the City by the Bay

Jon needed directions to Sacramento and was told to talk to a Chinese man who had told the miners that he'd jumped ship in San Francisco, traveled by river boat to Sacramento, and then attempted to mine gold on a river near a place with the odd name "Hangtown." Once there, the man had been informed, by a Chinese laundress, that if he wanted to avoid becoming one of the unwelcome "yellow claim jumpers" who were routinely hanged, then he had best be on his way to Chinese Camp.

The man said that his journey had taken him two months, and he had to cross four rivers whose headwaters were located in the High Sierras and were fed solely by melted snow. Because it had been late Summer, the four rivers were low and their temperature was not ice-cold like they were in the Spring. It was now early April, and Jon was assured he would not be able to travel from there to Sacramento by swimming across any of these rivers.

Moreover, because the valley that the four rivers flowed into was a tule reed-filled marshland, Jon was advised that he should return to San Francisco Bay by following the Southernmost river and then taking a riverboat to Sacramento. Since he had saved a good bit of money from his sailor's pay, Jon thought he could afford the fare for such a trip.

The sailor's jumper and trousers he had worn since leaving the ship were dirty and tattered. He had given up wearing traditional Chinese-style garb after he joined the ship's company and was given clothing that had formerly belonged to a sailor who was washed overboard in the Bering Sea during a fierce storm that had swept icy-cold waves of seawater over the ship's deck. He also sorely needed to replace the worn-out, low-top boots he'd been wearing since leaving Shanghai

Jon visited the many stalls and shops along Market Street in San Francisco. Finally, he decided to find a Chinese tailor, like his father, who could fit him with some fine, tailor-made, American-style clothing.

A Fine New Suit

Jon found a tailor's shop with a display of well-made clothing and decided to ask the tailor to make him a dark-colored, American suit. The tailor was quite pleased to accommodate his latest customer and immediately started to measure the young man for his fitting, after which he brought out a bolt of navy-blue, woven-wool fabric. Jon was concerned about the fact that it was wool and might not be able to be washed. The tailor went back and brought out a bolt of linen, advising him that not only was this fabric able to be washed, but it was also much more suitable for the hot weather that they would be experiencing as early as next month. The linen was died a dark-grey color, and the tailor said it would make the wearer a very well-dressed man when combined with a white shirt, black hat, tie, belt and shoes. Jon thought to himself, that when he was dressed in these clothes, he could even pass for a white man.

The next day, Jon paid for the suit, and after buying all of the accessories the tailor had suggested, he had just enough money for a meal and a one-way ticket for his passage on the riverboat to Sacramento. Jon decided to return to the ivory-carver's shop and return the wicker backpack and the other items the man had so generously given him.

He was offered lodging that night in the man's humble dwelling at the foot of a steep bluff near the wharves. He boarded the riverboat the next day. It crossed San Francisco Bay and steamed up the river delta, which was fed by the convergence of the waters from the Calaveras, Mokelumne, San Joaquin, and the Sacramento Rivers, as it carried Jon toward his next adventure.

Early Sacramento

Jon arrived in Sacramento and saw a posted sign that read:

NOTICE:

THE CENTRAL PACIFIC RAILROAD IS INTENDING TO HIRE AS MANY ABLED-BODIED MEN AS IT CAN TO AID IN THE CONSTRUCTION OF A RAILROAD LINE ACROSS THE UNITED STATES! APPLY NOW AT THE CP'S SACRAMENTO BUSINESS OFFICES IN THE CROCKER BUILDING AT FIFTH & B STREETS

NOTE: ONLY WHITES NEED APPLY

Jon immediately walked to the Crocker Building, and after a long wait, was ushered into the office of Mister John Strobridge, the railroad's Construction Manager. Strobridge was quite impressed with Jon's well-dressed appearance. After he'd asked what kind of job Jon wanted, he was somewhat surprised with the bold answer, "The kind that will pay the best!"

After interviewing Jon and learning that he could not only read and write, but he was also schooled in mathematics, Strobridge decided to hire him as his assistant at a salary of fifty dollars per month. As he was entering Jon's name in his payroll ledger, he spelled it John Hahn. When Jon told him it was actually spelled

Jon Han, Strobridge exclaimed, "You're Chinese!"

Jon replied, "My father was, but my mother was White."

After hearing this, and learning that Jon spoke both Mandarin and Cantonese, as well as perfect English, Mister Strobridge said he needed to take him to meet Mister Crocker.

Why Not Hire the Chinese?

On the way to Crocker's Office, Jon was told that the man he was going to meet with had the foolish idea that their railroad should hire Chinese laborers to grade the way and lay track, but Strobridge said he really had strong doubts that the Chinese men were strong enough.

"Have you never heard about the Great Wall of stone that the Chinese people built all the way across China?" Jon asked.

Strobridge replied, "Funny thing about that. Mister Crocker asked the members of the U.S. Congress the same thing!"

After Jon was introduced, Crocker told him that he intended to hire as many Chinese laborers as he could to help build the railroad. This was because they had managed to hire only a handful of White men who had applied, and those men had only managed to lay track a short distance across the Sacramento Valley and stopped at the first granite cliff they had come to in the Sierras

Crocker said, "At that rate, the Union Pacific Railroad, which was rapidly building their line West from Nebraska, will be loudly knocking on the Central Pacific's door in no time at all!"

Mr. Crocker also told Jon that one of his partners in the enterprise was Mr. Leland Stanford who, when he was selected to be president of the Central Pacific, made the statement in his inaugural speech, "All of the Chinese in California should be deported and shipped back to China!"

"Well, I intend to prove him wrong, and *you* are going to help me do it!" Crocker loudly proclaimed.

Jon was given the assignment of recruiting as many as ten to fifteen thousand Chinese laborers who were to be paid a wage of twenty-five dollars per month. In addition to his salary of fifty dollars a month, Jon would be paid one dollar for each Chinese worker he hired.

Jon was thrilled to hear that he might earn more than ten thousand dollars—a fortune in those days. So it seemed that he had finally arrived at his own personal version of "Gold Mountain!"

7 ❖ The Russian

Karl Paudowski's father was a Lithuanian carpenter who had met and married a very beautiful Ukrainian woman. After one year had passed, the young couple decided to move to Moscow, where their son Karl was born. As a young man Karl had learned the carpentry skills from his father that he would need to make a living on his own. At the age of eighteen, he was told there was a demand for carpenters in Vladivostok to build not only sailing vessels, but also the houses and shops to support the growing population there. So he decided to strike out on his own for that distant settlement.

Karl knew a lot more about building houses than he did about boats and ships, and he made a good living by building living quarters and warehouses at the port of Vladivostok. Because he had been raised in a family with a strong Russian Orthodox religious indoctrination, he did not waste any of his money on drinking or the loose women who frequented the saloons near the docks.

After only two years of hard work, he managed to save quite a bit of money, and contributed much of that to his father and mother who had decided they wanted to relocate back to Lithuania and start raising chickens.

Off to Alaska

Shortly thereafter, Karl learned there was a demand for carpenters in the newly created fishing and fur trapping village of Sitka, Alaska. In fact, the new settlement had need of a good carpenter with the skills to construct a Russian Orthodox Church, which would be topped with the traditional onion-shaped spire on top. Karl knew that he had the skills to do this, and bought passage on the next sailing vessel bound for Alaska.

It turned out to be a very rough voyage across the shallow Bering Sea. Since he'd never even been aboard any vessel in his life, Karl found himself horribly seasick, as the vessel wallowed over the high waves during the crossing. Four days later, when he staggered off the vessel and onto the dock at Sitka, Karl still had the odd sensation that the ground beneath him was rocking back and forth, mimicking the motion of the ship out at sea.

Karl was feeling much better the next morning. Following a hearty breakfast at the boarding house where he had secured a room, Karl headed for the middle of the small village where the stone foundation was being laid for the start of construction for a small church. Karl was directed by a worker to see the priest who was supervising the work to inquire about being hired. After assuring the priest that he was a loyal follower of the Russian Orthodox religion, his newest employment was soon secured.

St. Michael's Cathedral, Sitka, Alaska

There had been no plans drawn up for the spire on the church, but Karl knew just how he intended on building it after the rest of the church was completed. He had seen how the shipbuilders in Vladivostok had steamed and curved the wooden beams and planks for the construction of sailing ships. The entire island of Sitka was covered in a thick forest of Spruce trees, and Karl knew that spruce wood would be ideal for creating the curved upright beams and circular bows required to support the curved outside planks of the spire. All he needed was to provide the local sawyers with the detailed instructions for cutting the wood into the exact shapes and sizes that he would need. Once that was completed, he built a steaming shed and arranged to have some local men employed to tend the fires and wet the wood, so it could be bent into the curved shapes he needed to complete the dome.

Because of the extremely moist climate of Sitka, Karl decided that the church should be built without the use of cast iron spikes and nails. While the moisture would not harm the spruce wood, it would cause any cast iron fastenings to rust away. Because this structure was intended to last at least several lifetimes—Karl decided to fasten all of the wood together with spruce pegs. Karl hired an apprentice to painstakingly drill all of the holes and carve the pegs so that they would all fit perfectly when Karl drove them in with his mallet.

Off Again—This Time to California

Of course, it took far longer to build the church than it did to build the same size structure in Vladivostok. Consequently, by the time the church was finished, all the other buildings in Sitka had been completed, and there was no longer a need for a carpenter of Karl's skills there. Karl decided he could return on the next vessel bound for Russia, but he learned that far to the South of Alaska, on the North coast of the Pacific Ocean, was a place called California.

It was 1812, and was advised by a seaman that the Russian-American Fur Company was planning on building a Fort and a dock there to support the new trade in sea-otter pelts and to supply the traders and nearby settlers with food and manufactured goods. Karl was told that carpenters were needed for this project, so Karl he decided to book passage on the next coastal steamer heading South.

The next vessel to arrive in Sitka unloaded a cargo of dried codfish before it was set to sail on to Northern California with a cargo of spruce lumber. The vessel's owner agreed to take on a passenger, and Karl booked his passage. Once Karl boarded the vessel, he was not pleased with the accommodations. They were not very clean and quite small. The boat was not even large enough to be called a ship. It had previously been a fishing-net trawler, converted into a small coastal steamer. It reeked of salted codfish, the deck planks were grimy and oily, and the deckhands seemed to be just as filthy. There were two stacks of wooden clubs on the deck that were blood-stained, and they appeared to have been used to club something to death.

Karl was told they were headed to Fort Ross and after the lumber was unloaded, the crew would be hunting for fur seals or sea otters. Sea otter pelts were highly valuable, and the mammals were being hunted nearly to extinction off the coast of Russia. Karl was told that as the boat approached them, curious otters would swim near to take a look at it. Then, the men with clubs would lean over the side with their clubs, and even if the poor creatures attempted to swim out of harm's way, they would be brutally clubbed and hauled aboard and skinned, sometimes while still alive. Then, their skinless bodies were thrown back into the sea.

Another mammal the otter hunters regularly killed and ate was the sea cow, related to the manatee. Large numbers of these animals were killed and eventually, none of their species would survive the hunting. The talk of slaughter disturbed Karl, and he could hardly wait to get off the vessel.

When Karl arrived at Fort Ross, he learned that construction had already begun. The fort was being built entirely of local coastal redwood logs, and the outer walls surrounding the perimeter were smaller redwood tree trunks, much like the wood stockades around the outside of old military forts. Karl was unsure who the Russian-American Fur Company thought they had to defend themselves against, because he'd been told that the members of the local Pomo tribe were peaceful. Also, the Spaniards who occupied most of California had apparently chosen to not advance to the North of their last mission, which was many miles to the south in San Rafael.

Because even the structures inside the stockade were being built of small redwood logs, Karl was told the only need for a carpenter of his skill would be to building doors and window shutters and to split shingles to cover the roofs. He accepted and was soon well occupied with these tasks.

Fort Ross, California Coast, 1828

Down the Coast to a New Beginning

It wasn't long before Karl finished the work on the fort and was ready to move on to another place where his services would be needed. The cook at the fort, who spoke Russian, had come to California from the shores of the Black Sea and served as a crewman on a whaler for two years in the Pacific Ocean. He advised Karl that there was great demand in San Francisco for wooden barrels and kegs that could be used for liquids such as whale oil, wine, and vinegar, as well as fresh water for ships. A man who could make wooden barrels would surely earn a good income there.

This was all itt took to convince Karl to pack up and start traveling South for the opportunity.

Karl was so anxious, in fact, to start making his way to San Francisco, that he was unwilling to wait for the next ship to arrive at Fort Ross. There was no way to tell when the next ship would arrive or whether it would be sailing to San Francisco or returning to Russia. So, Karl decided to start hiking South and shortly, he was passing through beautiful groves of coastal spruce, fir, and finally, large groves of redwood trees.

Those evergreens grew so high that he had to tilt his head back so far that it stretched his neck muscles as he strained his eyes to see their tops in the bright sunlit sky above. There were a few coastal streams leading to the sea, where he was able to spear some trout. Both the Eel and the *Russka Ryaka* (Russian River) were full of silver salmon that were heading upstream in their Fall spawning run. As he finally started to approach the area north of San Francisco Bay, he started seeing some numerous groves of live oak trees. He was sure that their wood would make fine barrel staves.

Karl found some fishermen sitting near the bay

shore and, after offering to replace a broken plank in their boat that had been damaged when it hit some rocks near the shore, Karl persuaded them to give him a ride across the wide bay. It was slack tide when they ferried him across the great bay. There was a strong wind gusting from the West and it brought with it a damp, cold fog that reminded Karl of a Winter's day.

It was early September, and the weather on the peninsula leading down from the Spanish Mission in San Rafael had been extremely warm. The fisherman said there was an icy-cold offshore current that ran down the West Coast all the way from Alaska to Chile. In the Summer, there was frequently a fog bank lingering a mile or two off the coastline. If a westerly wind blew toward the shore, there would be a wide bank of fog moving all across the expanse of the bay. Whenever this occurred, a Summer day in San Francisco could resemble something like Winter.

Shortly after Karl was settled in San Francisco, he bought a city lot close to the shore of the bay, then built a large building using redwood lumber cut from the nearby forests across the bay. He then started producing oak barrels and kegs. He employed a blacksmith, who had a shop nearby to produce the iron bands that held the curved oak staves together, and he also employed an apprentice. He named his firm The Golden Gate Cooperage Company. The company was highly successful, and Karl eventually built a mansion on top of a hill that is now named Russian Hill.

Virginia City, Nevada

8 ❖ The Silver Strike

At the top of the Virginia foothills, located to the Northeast of Carson City, Nevada, sits the town of Virginia City. It is now a tourist attraction, but it was once the site of a vast, buried treasure that was pulled from the earth.

By the 1860s, there were many individuals and companies that were engaged in prospecting for gold and silver at the top of what folks called "Gold Hill," a place that would later grow to be one of the many "boomtowns" in the West. Two years after the Civil War broke out, Nevada was admitted to the Union in order to gain access to the gold and silver that they sorely needed to keep financing the war. Between 1860 and 1880, Virginia City mines yielded 6,971,641 tons of ore, valued at $14,000,000 for the gold and $21,000,000 for the silver. In today's dollars this would amount to billions.

Gold Hill, late 1870s

Logging off the timber needed for shoring up the interior of the mines resulted in the total deforestation of thousands of acres of pines in the Sierras many miles West of what became known as "The Comstock." The many hundreds of acres of tall pines that now grow in the mountains surrounding Lake Tahoe are all "second growth" forest.

A railroad was built primarily to transport supplies for the Comstock and to haul ore out to the smelters. It was named The Virginia and Truckee, but the line never actually reached the town of Truckee in the Sierra Nevada Mountains. The V & T had a connection with the Central Pacific Railroad (later the Southern Pacific) at Reno, Nevada and its tracks crossed the Truckee River over a short railroad bridge just yards East of the Lake Street Bridge in Reno (The town once known as Lake's Crossing before being named for a Civil War general.)

Stopping Short of His Destination

Jim Townsend Junior stopped the mule he was riding, turned and looked up into a canyon that ran uphill to the North. The wagon train he was riding alongside had been headed due West, toward the Sierra Nevada Mountains. The members of the train had broken camp early this morning alongside a grove of willows and cottonwood trees that were growing next to the Carson River. It had been a chilly night, but now in the daytime, the bright sun was becoming increasingly hot and it beat down on his neck and back.

It was amazing how the high desert air of Nevada could heat the desert so intensely in the daytime and yet turn so frigid at night. In his hometown in Iowa, an extremely hot day meant a hot night, unless a thunderstorm rolled in with a burst of welcome cooling air. The folks on this wagon train had not had any rain to relieve them since they had double-teamed their oxen to struggle up to the crest of Idaho's Humboldt Mountains.

That day, a heavy rain fell and filled its waters that fed a river of the same name. It was the one that flowed South from the top of those mountains and turned West at their base, only to sink into the sands of the desert at the place folks called the Humboldt Sink.

Even though he had joined the wagon train when it departed Council Bluffs, Iowa, bound for California, and had served as one of their hunters, Jim suddenly felt a desire to leave the wagon train here. He was many miles short of his intended destination— the foothills of the Sierras, where gold had been dis-covered when he was a very young child. But Jim now had a strong feeling that he should leave the train and explore this canyon. It led towards a high range of hills and narrowed as it sloped toward the top. A small stream trickled down the center of the canyon, and it appeared likely that gold may have washed down from the mountaintop.

He bid farewell to Mister McLeary, the old wagon master who had been leading wagon trains westward since the 1850s, then turned his mount, named Jenny, and Jimmy, the pack mule his Pa had named after him, toward the canyon. As they climbed, Jim saw that he was not alone in thinking this canyon might be a source of loose (or placer) gold. He could see the shapes of nu-merous canvas tents pitched on both sides of the canyon and many men digging in the dirt on both sides of it. Sluice boxes were set up in the creek, which was now a muddy trickle down the hill. He continued to urge Jenny up the grade that steepened as she plodded along, but Jenny plainly did not want to make this climb. Jim had to keep pulling hard on the lead rope to keep the stubborn animal moving. Jim recalled how his father always had to yell and cuss at Jenny when the two mules were teamed up to pull a plow or wagon back home. His father often swore that he would take a two-by-four to the mule someday and beat him senseless, but he never did. Jim always believed that Pa secretly admired Jimmy for his strength, in spite of his balky nature. When Pa gave Jim the two mules to take on his Westward journey, he said Jenny was the mule to ride and Jimmy was the one he should load up with all his belongings.

Turning to Hunting

Besides the mules, Jim's Pa had given him the old Kentucky rifle that had belonged to his grandfather. The old man had left his home near the border of West Virginia to settle in Ohio many years ago. The rifle had originally been handmade as a flintlock by a fine gun-smith, but Pa had it modified to use percussion caps after they were invented. It had a beautiful, cherry-wood stock that each past owner had hand rubbed with linseed oil that darkened it to a chestnut color. Many of the metal parts were case-hardened and gleamed with hues of blue, green and black, and there was never a speck of rust allowed to pit the barrel. The rifle shot only a .36 caliber ball, which was meant to hunt smaller game.

However, the small bore contributed to its accuracy, and when Jim hunted with it, he could shoot the head off a turkey and take down a standing deer by hitting just behind the ear, so he didn't ruin any of the meat. It was this rifle, and his skill with it, that allowed Jim to sign on as a hunter and earn his keep on the wagon trail West.

He'd he left his home in Marietta, Ohio with very little money to travel to California to seek gold. His wealth consisted only of a handful of small silver coins and a few crumpled paper notes issued by the Bank of Cincinnati. After he arrived at the first sluice he came to, Jim asked a miner if he had been able to find any gold.

The miner replied, "Some, but just enough to keep me working this spot. Some of those others located uphill are finding more. That's why everyone calls this place Gold Hill!" Now, if you're looking to mine, you'll have to travel a lot higher, and to do that you'll have to mine without any water. This here creek flows out of the side of the mountain about a mile up. Above that, you'll not be able to sluice and will have to take up hard rock mining. But who knows, you just might hit the vein of quartz that this loose gold comes from, and that's called the mother lode. You will need lots of tools for that kind of digging."

"All I have is a shovel. Where would I be able to get a pickaxe?" Jim replied.

The miner explained, "There's a trading post located in a tiny settlement named Genoa, about eight miles West of here. It's run by some Italian fellow and, I tell you, he charges some really high prices. Of course, most tools come from the East Coast and have to be carried by sailing ship around Cape Horn to San Francisco, then travel by riverboat to Sacramento, and finally be hauled by horse and wagon over Carson Pass. So, most of the price goes to pay for all that transportation."

Jim replied "Well, I have very little money, so hard rock mining may be beyond my means, but I'll ride ahead just to see what's up there before giving up."

As Jim rode further up the hill, he encountered many more sluices, some of which he was told had been successful at separating a fair quantity of loose gold from the mud and gravel. All of the ground on each side of the little creek had been staked out as claims, so it appeared he'd be out of luck when it came to setting up a sluice box. Jim and his two mules continued uphill. As the grade became even steeper, the color of the soil above where the water was flowing out of the side of the hill changed. It was a yellow-gray, color as opposed to the reddish-brown color of the soil he'd seen down the hill.

Then Jim spied a cave located on the side of the hill. The opening was framed in hand-hewn timber. It was a hard rock mine! When he rode closer to the opening, a man appeared from the shaded entrance. He was quite tall and had a reddish beard streaked with gray.

He called out, "Hello there mule rider! What brings you up to our mining claim?"

Jim replied, "I am just looking over the ground. All the sites downhill were staked out, and I was told that above the spring down there it would only be hard-rock mining. But I don't have any tools except a shovel. What else would I need?"

"Well, you will need a lot more than that! At the very least, you will need a rock drill, sledge hammer, blasting powder, a pick and a kerosene lantern, in addition to your shovel. You would also need some knowledge regarding where to start digging, a mine cart to haul the ore out of the mine, and if you find any ore, you would need a rock-crusher."

"I don't see any crusher here." Jim remarked.

"That's because we've not found any ore that needs to be crushed. When we do, samples have to be taken to an assayer in Sacramento before we find out if we need to do any crushing and smelting. Hard-rock mining takes a lot of skill, money, hard work, and luck!"

Jim asked, "And where did you get the skill?"

"My brother and I mined zinc in Cornwall. That's in England, in case you never heard of it. Our father was a miner who emigrated from Norway to Cornwall, married, and settled there. We started mining when I was only fifteen years old and my brother was fourteen."

"Interesting. Where is your brother now?" Jim asked.

"He went to Genoa to buy some food to carry us through to next week. The Italian charges us miners a lot for food, but we have nowhere else to get any!"

"It sounds like I could make more money hunting and selling the meat to the miners for some of their gold than I would trying to start mining."

"You could. And I know we would be pleased to buy fresh meat from you. What's your name?"

"It is Jim Townsend, Jr., but you can just call me Jim. Not Jimmy, because that is what I call my pack mule. What's your name?"

"George Groesch, and my brother's name is Robert. Now, if you want us to be your first customers for fresh meat, why don't you set up your tent near ours. The water flowing from the spring down the hill is good, but you will taste some minerals in it. If you boil it in a pot, the salt remaining in the bottom will likely be a treat for your mules."

"I will try that. They deserve a treat after the hard work they were put through on this long journey."

"Why did you decide to ride a mule instead of a horse?" the miner asked.

"Well, Jenny, the mule, I rode most of the way from Marietta, Ohio, was part of a team that my father gave me. I had no money to buy a horse, but I can tell you that it was a good decision to ride Jenny. She has a steady walking gait and there were few, if any, places that I required her to run. Also, a mule is far more sure-footed over rough ground or a narrow, rocky trail than a horse. Mules are smart, and they won't even approach a rattlesnake, bear, or cougar, while a horse is just as likely to bolt when coming upon one. When I hunt, Jimmy has no problem with my draping a bloody carcass across his back, something that some pack-horses will not even tolerate. So, I have no problem with mules."

After pitching his tent, Jim decided to continue up the mountain to see if he could spot any wild game.

There was a wide vista at the top, and he saw a small herd of desert sheep grazing on the side of a large hill. In order to reach them, he would have to cross a deep valley, but if he went that way he would surely be spotted. He decided that he could head north, skirt around the valley and approach them from the backside of the hill. That would take quite a while, and he hoped the herd would still be there when he topped the hill. However, it was still early in the day, and if he was lucky, he could shoot at least one. His plan worked, and he harvested a fat yew.

It was after dark when Jim returned with his kill. The two brothers had already started their evening campfire, which helped Jim spot their camp as he headed down the mountain. Even if they had not made a fire, Jenny would have smelled the spring some fifty yards downhill from their camp. After he greeted the brothers, Jim unloaded the sheep carcass and led the mule downhill for a drink.

George said, "This yew will make a huge mutton stew that we can all enjoy. Robert was able to buy some carrots and turnips from the Italian, and he can start boiling them after I go fetch a pot of water. Why don't you pour yourself a cup of coffee, Jim?"

"Thanks, I would like that. Since you are supplying the vegetables for the stew and sharing it and your coffee with me, I'll gladly donate the meat. Tomorrow, I plan to try to find the same herd again, and if I bag one perhaps trade some meat to a number of miners down there for a bit of their gold."

"Well, gold or silver are the accepted mediums of exchange here in the West. If you have any bank notes issued by some Eastern bank, I am afraid they are worthless here."

"I spent the last of my paper money in Council Bluffs for lead, powder and percussion caps, and have only a half dozen silver coins to my name. I will have to survive on my hunting skills as long as I can."

"That won't be a problem here on Gold Hill, or in any gold camp down in California. The folks engaged in mining gold have little time to devote to hunting."

"Good enough. By the way, George, have you or Robert seen any deer around?"

"Not many. You'll find many more if you travel West a dozen miles or so to the base of the mountains and about six miles South of Genoa. Of course, there may be a few deer right near Genoa. Robert told me he has seen some when he goes to the Italian's store.

The next day, Jim struck his tent, loaded it and his cooking utensils on the pack saddle on Jimmy, saddled Jenny and set off for the base of the mountains to the west. He decided to bring only what he would need to spend a night or two, but he was really not sure how long this hunt would take. He figured that he would camp near where he planned to hunt before returning to Gold Hill with one or two deer.

It was around noon when he arrived at the Italian's store where he spent his last silver coins on some percussion caps. There were no other folks there, and the Italian welcomed his companionship and offered

Jim some lunch, which consisted of slices of a spicy hard salami and white cheese. The cheese was harder and drier than the white cheese his mother used to make. The Italian said that Italians in San Francisco made both, which could be stored for a long time without spoiling. Jim wished he had enough money to buy some of each, and decided that after he'd traded enough fresh meat to the miners for some gold, he would come back and do just that.

That evening, he set up camp in a valley at the base of the nearby mountains that were bisected by the Carson River. He knew the thick groves of willows growing near the river banks would be a great attraction for deer, who loved to feast on their tender new growth. Jim was sure that at dusk all the deer would be leaving their beds, where they usually spent the warm afternoon, and would be coming to the riverside to drink and then feed the whole night.

He laid down behind a large, fallen cottonwood tree and waited. He was able to shoot one young buck that evening and the next morning took down a large doe. After dressing out the doe, he broke camp, loaded both of the deer on old Jimmy, and set off for Gold Hill.

This time, he followed the Carson River as it wound its way to the Northeast through a huge valley and was able to reach Gold Hill before the miners had quit their labors for the day. Jim started cutting all the meat into meal-sized portions for trading. The trades with the miners went well, and Jim knew he had a ready market for his game.

The Groesch brothers kept on with their hard-rock mining but never had any luck on their search for white quartz that might have veins of gold running through it. It was mid-October, and they were running short of funds and thought they might have to spend the Winter in Sacramento, either working at a smelter or unloading riverboat cargo. Jim decided that he might spend the Winter right here if the other miners stuck it out.

A Strike at Last, But Then a Tragedy

One day George brought a piece of grey rock back to their camp and started to pound it with his rock hammer. After he had crushed the rock, he exclaimed, "My God, this is silver ore! We have dumped tons of it just outside the opening of the mine. I need to run back to the mine and tell Robert to stop dumping it until we can get some to Sacramento for an assay."

Just then, they heard a scream from the mouth of the mine. When they got there, they found Robert holding onto his foot and writhing on the ground in agony. George asked, "What's wrong, Robert! What happened to your foot?"

"My pick glanced off a rock and came down hard on my foot. It punched through my boot and went into my foot. It feels like it went all the way through it!" After they removed the boot, Jim saw that it was full of blood, and the pickaxe had indeed nearly gone all the way through his foot.

Jim asked, "Is there a doctor anywhere near here? That wound needs attention right away!"

George replied, "There's no doctor around here. We will have to care for Robert here and doctor him ourselves."

The puncture wound was large, and there was also some foreign matter clinging to it. George heated some water to wash it, while Jim carefully removed threads of a rather dirty wool sock from the edge of the wound. Then, after George washed the wound, he tore a sleeve off a cotton shirt and bound it tightly around Robert's foot. Robert didn't sleep that night as a result of the pain.

The next morning, they found that the bleeding had stopped but the area around the wound was badly swollen and bright red. The foot was hot to the touch and he had a high fever as well. George told Jim that he thought the wound had become infected, but they had nothing to treat it with. Jim said he would get to Genoa as fast as Jenny could carry him and see if the Italian had anything they could use as a disinfectant.

After Jim reached the trading post, he learned that the only thing the Italian had to use for a disinfectant was a pint bottle of whiskey. Jim paid him with the brothers' last bit of cash and set off back to Gold Hill as quick as he could. When Jim returned to the camp, George opened the whiskey and poured some over the wound.

Robert yelled, "My God that hurts! Give me the rest of that bottle to drink and kill the pain." George gave Robert the remaining whiskey, but he soon regretted it, as Robert quickly drained the small bottle.

"Now we'll have nothing more to use on your wound," George exclaimed. "Let's hope the wound doesn't turn septic or you may lose that foot!" In the days that followed, the lack of anything to disinfect the wound proved to be a real problem. The fourth day the skin around the wound had turned blue-green and oozed pus. Two days later, there were dark streaks running up from the wound halfway up to Robert's knee.

George told Robert "I am afraid you have blood poisoning and that leg will have to come off!"

Robert cried out, "If it has to come off it will, but it will *not* be done without the services of a real doctor!"

Unfortunately, the nearest doctor was on the opposite side of the Sierra Nevada Mountains, and there were no means of transportation available except Jenny, and Robert was in no shape to ride. Construction of the Central Pacific Railroad was still underway, but had progressed only fifty miles west of Sacramento.

Robert's fever grew worse each day and his wound caused his foot and leg to swell to almost twice it's normal size. George and Jim did everything they could to keep Robert comfortable, but they decided he would probably be gone before the month of November arrived. He passed away on October 29th. They held a small funeral and placed a wooden marker with Robert's name carved on it on the burial mound on top of Gold Hill.

On to Sacramento

As they had in 1846—the year the Donner Party became trapped—heavy snows had completely blocked their route over the mountains by the next day. However, the two men had no idea this had happened.

George asked Jim if he would come with him to take his sample of silver ore to Sacramento for the assay and bring Jimmy along to carry whatever he thought they would need to cross the Sierra Nevada mountains. Because he still planned to eventually make his way to California, Jim agreed, and they started packing that evening. They made a list of everything they would need, including a tent, food, water, a frying pan and cook pot, canvas sleeping bags, two wool blankets, long underwear, all of their wool socks, scarves, and heavy mittens. Of course, Jim decided he would bring along his treasured Kentucky rifle, and all of the lead, powder and the few percussion caps that he had left.

After Jim left Jenny in the care of a miner who agreed to look after her for the Winter, they set off early the next day. There was a heavy wind blowing through the mountain passes and storm clouds were on the Western horizon. By the time they had crossed the Carson Valley, the snow was coming at them horizontally. The two men had to keep their heads tipped down and could barely see a few feet ahead of them.

George declared, "This weather really does not bode well for our crossing of Carson Pass!"

Conditions grew even worse as they reached the valley where Jim had slain the two deer. The wind shrieked as it funneled through the narrow river valley and the snow was blowing so hard that the two men could not even see more than a few feet in front of their faces.

Every time the two stopped to get their bearings to make sure they were still headed toward the pass, Jimmy would turn his tail to the wind and balk at being turned around to face it again. In fact, Jim practically had to drag the mule forward with the lead rope attached to his halter.

"I swear, carrying the packs myself might be easier than dragging this mule into the wind!" Jim shouted. Of course, considering the weight of the packs, that would hardly even be possible.

The two men decided to camp for the night in a grove of pines at the head of the valley near the place the Carson River stopped cascading down the side of the mountain and leveled off for its entry into the valley. It was not easy to set up the tent, since the trunks of the high pines did little to break the roaring wind. The two men were finally able to complete their difficult task and crawl inside the tent for the night. They ate a cold supper of deer jerky, because building a fire in the storm would have been impossible. The wind continued to roar down the pass and the tent flapped violently all night, which made it difficult to sleep. George guessed the storm would ease up around dawn, and that, hopefully, they would wake up to a sunrise that signaled its passing. He was very wrong.

The two men broke camp early the next morning, eager to make their way up the pass before conditions got even worse. It took all morning to struggle up the first steep grade that ran alongside the river and zigzagged all the way down the steep hill. By noon, they had reached a high valley where the Carson River meandered across it to the waterfall that dropped down into the narrow passage they had just exited.

"We might be able to build a fire and make some soup with the deer jerky that we have left," said Jim.

George replied, "Well, we can surely try. If the weather keeps up like this, we may have little hope for a hot meal tonight."

Relief from a Stranger

The two men finally found enough shelter from the wind behind a thick grove of small willows alongside the river. This enabled them to make a fire and cook some deer-jerky soup for a warm, noontime meal. This warmed them considerably, and they decided to make an early camp there and spend the night. This would allow them to rest up for the steep climb over the pass that lay ahead.

That evening, when they were contemplating what they could use to make their dinner or breakfast the next morning, they saw a native approaching their camp from the North. The man was carrying a huge bundle wrapped in a deer hide, and the two white men grew more and more curious as he approached as to what its contents might be. They signaled for the Indian to come and join them by the fire, and when he set down his bundle they were able to see that it contained many dried fish. These were very large fish and George said folks calledthem "salmon trout." Even though the fish had been smoked and their overall color was a yellowish-brown, George and Jim could see the colorful slash of reddish-orange on their throats that later would earn them the name "cutthroat trout."

The Washoe Native pulled three large, smoked fish from his bag and handed one to each of the white men, signing for them to eat. All three enjoyed the fish as their evening meal. George signed to inquire where the fish had come from by using his hand to mimic a swimming fish and pointing to the North. The native said, "Da ho," and signed that there was a very large and deep body of water to the Northwest. He also signed to indicate he wanted to know where the two

"Da ho," Lake Tahoe, California

men were heading, and George pointed to the West and up the hill in that direction and then mimicked walking with his fingers. The Washoe shook his head to indicate that the snow was quite deep ahead on Carson Pass.

George pointed North and asked, "Da ho?" and mimicked walking up and over the mountains. The native shook his head no to let them know this also was not a good route. Then the Washoe pointed North and signed to simulate the passing of four moons to the North and then walking up and down mountains to a large valley below and smiled. Then he pulled two fish from his pack that would provide another meal for the two Whites. Jim hoped they would be able to spear some of the same kind of fish in the large lake the Native had called "Da ho," but when they reached it, they found the edge of the lake was covered with a coating of ice that was too thin to walk on, and the water was so clear that the fish spied them when they waded out beyond the ice in an attempt to spear one.

Survival?

The two men made their way along the East side of the huge lake. It was a two-day journey, and they needed to break through snowdrifts to travel, at best, an exhausting five miles each day. They discovered a river that flowed from a shallow cove at its Northwest end. The river headed to the North, and they followed it for two days, before it turned toward the East and flowed down into a canyon. The sides of the canyon were as steep as any they had ever seen and covered with deep snow, so they could only turn and follow the river downhill. Was the Indian wrong about the distance to the place the mountains could be crossed? They had already slept through six nights. Perhaps, the Indian meant four weeks, or even four months, before they would reach a pass they could cross in Winter. Considering they'd had no food since the two dried fish the Indian had given them, Jim thought he would have to either find and shoot a deer soon, or they might have to slay and eat Jimmy.

It took another two days of struggling through deep snow to follow the river down to level ground where the windswept snow was only a few inches deep. To the East lay a large valley with a wide meadow, and at the north end, was a huge mountain. It was treeless and steep, but only about five hundred feet in elevation. Jim spied a half-dozen deer browsing on the brush growing on its sides about two hundred yards from them, and he decided to try to get close enough to get a shot at one. He asked George to set up camp and to hobble Jimmy at a nearby creek bank so he could browse on some sparse patches of bunchgrass growing amongst the willows.

It took most of the day to carefully stalk the deer because they kept moving toward the East side of the hill as they browsed. Jim had to crawl with his stomach and chest scraping the rocky ground in order to not alarm the deer. He was able to get within one hundred and fifty yards of the closest one before he decided to take a shot. He aimed at the very top edge of the buck's back, above the spot the heart and lungs would be, in order to compensate for the drop of the lead ball at that long distance. He took the shot, and the large buck dropped to it's knees. It was still alive, but Jim decided not to waste another shot. He laid down his rifle, took out his knife, jumped up and ran as fast as he could the entire distance between himself and the buck.

The wounded buck was still on its knees when Jim drew near, but it sprang to it's feet when he approached. When Jim was within twenty yards of the buck, which had an extremely full set of antlers, the deer charged him with its head down. It was fortunate that the animal had been severely weakened by the shot and wasn't able to charge very rapidly. Jim waited until the deer was nearly on him, then quickly side-stepped, grabbed the closest horn, twisted the buck's neck and slashed its throat just as it was passing alongside him.

It was quite late when Jim finished dressing the deer, so he made a fire and decided to spend the night before returning to where George waited below. That night a pack of coyotes came up the hill, yipping loudly and they made a quick meal of the offal that Jim had removed when he dressed out the buck.

Before dark, Jim took some time to admire the large animal he had bagged. The buck had a narrow black tail, rather than the wide white tail found on the deer in Iowa. Also, the bucks' ears were huge—almost as large as Jimmy's. Jim decided this deer must be what folks called a "mule deer."

The deer probably weighed about 120 pounds, which was more than Jim could carry. He decided he would have to drag the animal downhill, where he and George could build a fire and smoke the meat to make enough jerky to last them for the rest of their journey to Sacramento.

The next morning Jim returned to George's campsite at the creek dragging the large deer carcass behind him. It was fortunate that it was downhill all the way, and there were only a few ravines to skirt around. It obviously did not rain often in this part of the country, but when it did, it carved some deep landmarks.

George saw him coming and rushed up the hill to help drag the deer the last seventy-five yards. He was obviously upset and told Jim he had some very bad news.

Jim exclaimed, "What's wrong George?" His companion blurted out, "Some Indians stole Jimmy last night! I followed their trail this morning and then found his remains near the site of a large fire. They ate every bit of him! I swear, it must have been a whole tribe, so I guess it was lucky they were gone when I arrived, since I don't have a rifle!"

Jim cut willow branches to build a rack they could hang strips of venison on, and George gathered the dried wood they needed for a small fire to smoke the jerky. They roasted the liver for breakfast and boiled the heart all day to make a soup. They kept gathering wood to keep the fire under the racks of venison going that day, and were exhausted come nightfall. Both men slept soundly that night, but the next morning, they awoke to see that the wooden racks were empty.

George cried out, "Those thieving savages! They robbed us of all of we had to eat again!"

Jim thought it would be pointless to try to bag another deer out here and risk yet another raid. They cut some larger willow branches to make a travois they could drag behind them with the goods that Jimmy had been carrying on the packsaddle. Later that morning, they started off to the North with hopes that the Indian knew what he was talking about when he signed that they would be able to cross the mountains four moons North of the Carson River.

Over the Pass!

After traveling North for several days, they reached what looked like a low pass across the chain of mountains to the West. Of course, they had been climbing gradually as they made their way North, so even though the pass was high enough to have a deep snowpack, the way up to it was not that steep. They had not seen any deer since the one Jim had killed several days ago, and they were quite hungry. After they reached the top of the pass, Jim shot a lone muskrat he found swimming in the headwaters of a river that headed East down the steep side of the pass they were planning to take.

There was very little meat on the animal for them to share, so Jim decided to make a soup of it. They had no salt, so he flavored the soup with green-spruce needles, which gave it a bitter taste, but provided them with some vitamins.

At this point, George was totally exhausted by all of the rigors and exposure he had experienced throughout their journey. He confessed to Jim that when he was a young boy, he had a terrible fever, and he was told by a doctor that his heart would never be strong enough for a rigorous outdoor life. He insisted that he could go no further and asked Jim to leave him there. If he eventually felt better, he would try to make his way back down to the valley to the East and winter there.

George told Jim if he was able to make his way to Sacramento, then he could have the ore assayed and return to Gold Gulch the following Spring. Jim told George he should rest up that night and they would see how he felt the next morning. When Jim tried to wake George the next morning, he found the older man had expired soundlessley, and he hoped peacefully, in the night.

Jim covered the body some rocks he found at the edge of a stream bank, so the coyotes would not be able to consume the poor soul's remains. He then continued on his way Eastward, following the river all the way down to a large, grassy valley, and then headed South toward Sacramento.

Sacramento and the Assay at Last!

The assay results proved that the ore was rich with silver deposits. The mine site should be worth a fortune, considering the fact that tons of ore had already been mined and lay waiting for somebody to have it crushed and smelted. Jim knew he would have to find someone to finance the equipment to do this, and he roamed Sacramento for weeks that Winter trying to seek a partner who would provide the cash.

Every potential investor he asked was, at that time, already heavily invested in financing the hydraulic mining of gold in California, and none of them had any interest in putting money into a Nevada silver mine. When he returned to Gold Hill that Spring, Jim found that three men had taken over the site and were still trying to find a vein of quartz that might contain gold. He gave up any hope of ever becoming rich in the mining trade and decided to continue to earn his share of gold and silver by market hunting for miners.

After agreeing to provide the miner who cared for Jenny with free meat for the Summer, Jim hunted and exchanged meat for gold until he had a small fortune. He moved to Sacramento that Fall, bought a gun shop and hung his trusty Kentucky rifle on the wall behind the counter. When asked about it, he told folks, "That rifle earned my keep for years and this store as well!"

9 ❖ The Boomers

He was Irish to the bone, with red hair, freckles and all, born in Northern Ireland. His family had transplanted him six years prior, when they had immigrated to the town of Durham, in Northern England. He had been twelve then, but he was a strapping young lad of eighteen now, and restless to make his own way in the world.

His name was Archibald O'Reilly, but he thought that sounded a little too high-class, so he insisted that everyone call him Archie. Of course, he thought the

name Smith fit him much better, because he was a young blacksmith, as was his father, as well as both his grandfather and great-grandfather. Historically, in England, that was how you got your surname. If your distant ancestor had owned a bakery, for instance, your surname would have been Baker. A a man who hauled goods on a two-wheeled cart was named Carter. A woodworker would be named Carpenter. A man who carried luggage and trunks for the higher classes and royalty was named Porter.

Archie's best friend Ed, whom he'd gone to public school with, followed his father to work alongside him down in the coal mine in Sunderland after finishing his studies at the age of fourteen. This mine was hundreds of feet deep and ran out under the North Seas. They mined sea-coal, and after it was brought to the surface, it was loaded onto freighters sailing from the North Sea to ports all over the world.

Unlike Ed, Archie could not bear to think about descending into that black hole with thousands of tons of seawater just above the ceiling of sea coal, which was being removed each day. Just the thought of that ice-cold sea water rushing into the mine and filling your coal dust-blackened lungs terrified him.

Ed's surname was Shanks, not Miner. Ed always supposed that the family's naming predated the opening of the coal mines nearby. Ed used to joke about his name, saying he guessed he was a good runner because everywhere he traveled, he had to go by "Shanks mare." That is what folks called their mode of travel when they had no horse or money to ride a tram or train. He also joked that way back, one of his ancestors might have been the illegitimate son of King Edward Longshanks and had only been permitted to use the "back end" of the King's name.

Archie laughed when he heard that, "Imagine my lower-class parents naming me Archibald, like I was someday going to become a high and mighty Catholic bishop. And you, the son of a lowly coal miner, with maybe a bit of royal blood in your veins, being named Edward, after a king! Perhaps I should be after callin' you Sir Edward Shortshanks, the blooming Grand Duke of Edinburgh!"

"You do and you'll be wiping blood off your nose, you soddy potato eater!" Ed exclaimed.

The town of Durham was located in Northern England on the mainline of the Great Northern Railway that ran North from London, England to Edinburgh, Scotland. The O'Reilly's Blacksmith Shop was located just alongside the railway tracks. Everyone used to say it was on the wrong side of the tracks because the Durham Railway Station was on the other.

When he was a young lad, Archie was always fascinated by the huge huffing steam engine, and the loud squeal of the steel brake shoes against the driving wheels as the Engineer brought the great machine to a stop. Archie learned to spell Engineer in the second grade, and he'd always imagined he'd grow up to be one. Although, now that he had reached the age when he could apply for a job as a fireman, he learned that the only way you could get hired was if your father or an uncle was a member in good standing with the trainmen's labor union. So, he had to satisfy himself with just learning to be a smithy, like his father did when he was a young man.

"Flying Scotsman," Great Northern Railroad

Bound for America

One day, Ed told Archie that his Uncle Bob lived in America and he had offered to sponsor him if he traveled there. Bob had written to say that he'd discovered that America was indeed the land of opportunity, and he had been able to buy his own house in Brooklyn, New York with the wages he made working for a firm that produced wire rope and cables. Ed wrote a reply to his Uncle and asked if Archie might be able to come with him, if there was an empty bedroom in his house that they could both share for as long as it took them to find employment and earn enough money to get their own apartment. Bob sent his reply, saying both of them were welcome to share one of his bedrooms, but they would both have to absolutely guarantee that there would be no "hanky-panky" when they were living in the small house with his attractive sixteen-year old daughter and sharing the one bathroom. Ed wrote back promising that they both would respect his wishes in return for his generosity.

The two young men learned they could earn their free passage from Liverpool to New York City by signing on as firemen on any one of the ocean liners that were doing a good business transporting thousands of residents of England, Ireland and Western Europe to America. The two of them wasted no time in packing and boarding the first train headed for Liverpool.

The White Star ocean liner was a grand vessel, but the young men were destined to see very little of it on their voyage. The entire "black gang" was confined to the lowest deck in the ship for the entire voyage. Of course, their sweat-soaked and coal-dust blackened bodies were hardly in any shape to have been seen (or smelled), except by the other firemen. It was a blessed relief when the word came down that the ship had finally crossed the Atlantic, passed the "narrows," and made its entry into the Hudson River channel and turned toward the slips on the West side of Manhattan Island. The two young men had cleaned up as best they could, and made their way topside to disembark. Of course, this was only after all of the paying passengers had left the ship and their baggage was ashore.

All passengers without American passports had to board a ferryboat to Ellis Island for clearance by immigration officials. After this, the two young men hurried themselves to locate the Grand Central Railroad Station, where they were told they could purchase tickets on the Long Island Railroad. Uncle Bob had directed them to get off on the first stop, which was the Flatbush Avenue Station, and then take the Flatbush Trolley Car and get off at the corner of Flatbush and Fifteenth Street. Uncle Bob's house was within walking distance from the trolley stop, but they would have to wait until he got off from work, because his daughter was away at a music camp for the Summer.

Rather than spending the day sitting on the steps

of Uncle Bob's house, the two decided to explore the territory around Flatbush Avenue. They found a drug-store with an ice-cream parlor and both of them ordered what the "soda jerk" said was the best thing on the menu—a banana split. After they both had heartily consumed one, Ed ordered another. He said he had never tasted anything as wonderful as the combination of vanilla, chocolate, and strawberry ice cream with chocolate sauce and whipped cream on top of a split banana. Of course, because his father had minimal earnings, in their home, a treat like a small muffin or pastry was out of the question.

Ed had no mother and was unsure if she had died or run off when he was a baby. Nobody would ever speak of her, not even his aunt, who took care of him and his brother George. Of course, she was like a mother to the two of them and cooked a sweet bread pudding for them when she could spare some sugar.

Uncle Bob returned home that evening and wel-comed them to his small white clapboard house. Ed saw that the house had a small closed front porch that was encased with large glass windows. Half of the space inside was filled with large clay pots of what looked like tropical plants and there were rattan chairs to sit in and relax. He had never seen anything so exotic in his whole life! None of the homes in Durham or Sun-derland that he remembered had a closed-in porch, let alone tropical plants. This was only like something he had seen in a large garden park alongside the River Thames, when his family had taken a vacation trip to visit a relative in London.

Ed saw Uncle Bob was a bear of a man, and the last thing he would dare think of would be to trifle with his young cousin. Whether Archie would be able to resist her charms was another matter! Bob had huge hands and the thickest fingers he had ever seen—something Ed thought might have been a result of working at the wire-rope factory. Ed could imagine them around Archie's throat if he ever caught the lad sharing a kiss with his daughter!

One evening, Uncle Bob came home from work and told the young men there was a job opening at the factory for someone who knew something about working on machinery. That was something Archie thought he had the skills for, since he had apprenticed four years in his father's blacksmith shop, and went there the next day to apply.

Archie worked at the factory for several months, while Ed commuted to the city and worked for a jeweler stamping out what were supposed to be silver rings on a metal press that he actuated by stamping his foot down quite hard on a pedal. The so-called silver was actually pewter (a blend of silver and lead) that the jeweler highly polished to look like pure silver and sold at a profit. Neither of them liked their jobs, and both young men wanted to find other employment.

Archie especially wanted to get a job on one of the four railroads that ran into the island of Manhattan. These were the New York Central, the Pennsylvania, the New York, Hartford and New Haven, and of course, the Long Island Railroad. However, at that time, there were no open positions, because they had already been filled by either the sons, nephews, or cousins of members of the trainmen, locomotive engineers, firemen, or conductors' unions.

Off to Work for a Railroad

One day, a clerk at the New York Wire Rope Company with the prissy name of Percy told Archie he was going to call in sick the next day and take the ferry across the Hudson to Elizabeth, New Jersey and apply for a job as a payroll clerk with the Eire Railroad. The Eire was extending its line from central New Jersey to Buffalo, New York, and they were hiring on the spot.

Archie convinced Ed to come with him and the two took the ferry across the Hudson River to Elizabeth the next morning. Because Archie told the interviewer that he had training as a Blacksmith, he was given a job as a machinist and told he would travel with, and live on, their work train and make all of the necessary repairs to the Locomotive and any of the tools the track gang damaged. This suited him just fine, as it eliminated the need to pay for rented rooms. Ed was told he would be given a job as an apprentice car repairman, an occupation that employees of every railroad called "car-knockers." The two soon learned there were other nicknames used by railroad men. For example, they called a steam locomotive a "hog" and the nickname for a locomotive engineer was a "hoghead."

Soon, both men's days were filled with hard work as the roadbed was laid for the Eire Railroad's extended line. Their work hours were the customary twelve hours a day, six days a week. It took several days to get started, while everyone was occupied loading boxcars with hand tools and wooden kegs filled with railroad spikes, "fishplates" (used to anchor the rails to the wooden ties), and track joints (required to bolt two rails together). This took the better part of a day, after which the hard work began. All the steel rails and wooden railroad ties had to be lifted onto and stacked on flatcars. It took four men to lift and hoist a steel rail up to the height of the flatcar's deck, and two men to swing them onto the stacks on board. One man on each end of an oak crosstie was what it took to throw the heavy thing onboard.

The ties would then be placed in crisscrossed stacks and secured so they would not tumble around like "jackstraws" when the flatcars on the work train were jerked about when the train started forward or when it was braked to a stop. The work was exhausting and the men teamed up to take turns at heaving the heavy rails and ties on board.

Discovering Camp Shanks on the Hudson

Not much headway was made the first week, as everyone was learning their new jobs. That Sunday, the work train was idled and Archie said he was headed for the nearest "pub" (although they were not called that in New Jersey or anywhere else in the United States) to "hoist a few and look for a friendly local lass to fraternize with, if I get lucky!"

Ed did not drink and opted to take a hike to the East of them and look at the Hudson River from the tops of the "Palisades" on its West side. He soon learned they had not yet traveled far enough North to reach those high cliffs of sedimentary stone. He did, however, discover an empty Army camp located in a marshy area alongside the river. A lone guard told him that this was, of all things, Camp Shanks. The camp had been a staging area for the thousands of troops that were transported South on towed barges during the recent Civil war.

It seemed the slips on the West side of Manhattan Island had not been well suited for loading barges or for temporary housing for the troops that were waiting for the barges to return from the peninsula on the coast of Virginia, where troops had been assembled for the planned advance against what the guard said were called, "all of General Lee's damn Rebels," surrounding the state capital at Richmond. Archie told the guard that, believe it or not, his last name was Shanks. He left with some doubts that the guard believed him.

After the railroad tracks crossed the New Jersey state line and entered New York, the line laid out by the Eire's surveyors was starting to snake its way through the Catskill Mountains. A steam locomotive, especially one built in the 1800s, could not pull railcars up a steep grade, and the engineer in charge of the extension of the line desired that it not exceed four percent (that is, a four feet rise for one-hundred feet of track). There were a number of lakes to avoid, as well as rivers and streams that had to be bridged. Then, there was what Ed called those "bloomin' beaver dams" that the entire track gang would assemble to watch the team of explosive men place dynamite sticks in them to blow the logs, sticks and twigs the industrious mammals had woven and stacked together "all to smithereens," in Archie's words.

A Clear View to the West

The first Sunday after they had entered the Catskills, Ed decided to take a hike up to the top of a nearby hill that towered above the others. Because they were far from pubs (or local females), Ed was able to talk Archie into coming with him.

At first, Archie grumbled, "Why in the hell would I want to climb some damn steep hill, when I could just lie here on me bunk and cool my heels all day?"

Ed retorted, "Because it would be good for you!"

After climbing the hill, the two could see as far as the horizon to the West.

Ed said, "That's where I think the two of us should be heading. Did they teach you any geography in that heath-covered peat bog of a country you came from, and do you have any idea of how vast and varied this country is? There are wondrous things to the West of here and I, for one, intend to see them. So, are you coming with me or not?" Archie agreed with Ed, and the two were soon on their way up the next tallest hill to the East of them.

They took their time on their way up for a better view, in deference to Archie's lack of hill-climbing abilities. They also stripped and swam naked in a beautiful spring-fed lake halfway up the hill.

"Now if we had a couple of fair lassies with us, we'd be havin' a much better time, don't 'cha think?" Archie exclaimed.

"That's pretty much wishful thinking on your part Archie, but I admire your thought and wish it was so," was Ed's only reply.

Adirondack Mountains

They reached the top of the hill much later and found themselves gazine at a range of mountains to the West just before sunset. Scattered thunderheads rose above the mountains and the setting sun lit them with edges of gold. The openings of some of the thunderheads were highlighted with hues of pink and purple.

"Now there's a sight you won't be seeing in Durham or Sunderland!"

Ed explained, "That high ridge of mountains is part of the mountain chain named the Adirondacks. They run South along the Eastern United States until they terminate and the Appalachians begin. This country is full of fantastic mountain ranges. We had to memorize them in our sixth-grade geography class. I remember the ones in the center of the country are the Rockies and to the West are the Sierra Nevada, which I think is Spanish for snowy mountains. I am planning on someday climbing to the tops of both of those mountain ranges!"

The work on the rail line continued until they reached Buffalo, where they constructed an "interchange" that connected the Eire's tracks to the lines of the New York Central Railroad leading westward toward Chicago. Now that the connection between the two railroads was completed, a manufacturer in Newark, New Jersey could ship a boxcar load of his product by rail to Chicago, Illinois without having to have a "drayman" load the goods on his wagon, ferry it on a barge across the Hudson and transfer the freight into a boxcar at one of the NYC "team Tracks" in Manhattan.

Once the work was completed, the Eire laid off all its employees involved in laying the new line. They learned that they were not even going to be provided free transportation back to New Jersey. If they wanted to ride a passenger train back to New Jersey, they were expected to pay their fare, just like everyone else.

Both Archie and Ed had skills desired by every railroad company and were soon hired by the New York Central to work in their shops in Chicago. Both men appreciated that this would move them further to their ultimate destination in the West. Neither of the men cared much for the city of Chicago once they arrived there. The rail yard was located on the South side adjacent to the infamous Chicago River, into which the Chicago Stockyard employees tossed all of the offal from the hundreds of slaughtered cows and pigs each day. This putrid waste floated down the river where it emptied into Lake Michigan, where much of the city drinking water came from. Only the suburbs to the West were supplied with clean drinking water from deep wells.

Eventually, the city Engineers would have the river dredged to a depth lower than the lakebed, so the flow of the river would be reversed and the waste would be carried southward to the Ohio River and down the Mississippi to the Gulf of Mexico.

So, You're Boomers!

When the New York Central shop employees heard that Archie and Ed had been working for the Eire Railroad, they exclaimed, "We didn't know you two were both "boomers"!

Ed asked, "What's a boomer?" The shop worker replied, "That's a man who moves across the country working for one railroad after another."

Ed exclaimed, "Well then, I guess that makes us both boomers!"

A few weeks later, Ed confided in Archie that he didn't want to stay in Chicago another day. One of the men in the roundhouse told me the Milwaukee Road was looking for shop men in Milwaukee, Wisconsin, so let's be boomers and apply at their offices tomorrow."

What the machinist said was that the Milwaukee Road turned out to have the grandiose name The Chicago, Milwaukee, Saint Paul and Pacific. Ed really liked the sound of that, especially the Pacific part. They were hired that day, given a railway pass, and were on their way to Milwaukee that night.

Both men liked their new jobs at the Milwaukee Road, but several months later, they heard that there were job openings in Minneapolis, just across the Mississippi River from the Milwaukee Road station in Saint Paul. They learned that the Great Northern Railroad was planning on beginning an extension of their line all the way to Seattle in the state of Washington. When he heard this news, Archie exclaimed, "Imagine, of all things, they have a Great Northern Railroad right here in this country! Just like the rail line that runs through Durham!"

The Great Northern

What neither of the men were aware of was that the majority of the capital investment required for expansion of the rail lines throughout the United States in the late 1800s came from a number of wealthy English investors. At the start of America's great industrial revolution, buying stocks or bonds issued by a railroad that ran directly from Chicago, Illinois, located on the Western edge of what was then the industrial heartland of the United States, all the way to the West Coast, would be a good investment of capital for some wealthy Englishmen. This did not always prove to be the case when over-expansion of the rail lines to the

West occurred.

For example, the direct pathway to the Pacific Northwest would later be occupied by, not only the Great Northern, but also by the Milwaukee Road and Northern Pacific Railway, as well as indirectly by the joint route made possible by the interchanges in Nebraska, Utah and Oregon, which were the connection points between the Chicago and Northwestern, Union Pacific, Southern Pacific, and the Spokane, Portland and Seattle railroads. Waybills that accompanied railcars traveling over this circuitous route to Seattle used to read: C&NW-Omaha-UP-Ogden-SP-Portland-SP&S.

The fierce competition between the railroads operating over the four routes to the Northwest led to lower and lower revenues and profits, and falling stock prices, which brought serious financial consequences to their largest investors in England.

Joining in the Great Race to the Coast

So the boomers, tired of working the Milwaukee Road, traveled to Saint Paul using their Milwaukee Road employee passes, and then walked over a short bridge across the Mississippi, which was not very wide at its headwaters. They applied for employment with the Great Northern—or GN, as it was referred to by all.

Even though there were three railroads gearing up for a race toward the West Coast, the word on the street was that the Great Northern was the one with the capital needed to get started first and win one of the world's most difficult races. It was not the longest race. That was the race won in 1908, by a Thomas Flyer, the one and only American automobile of the four competitors in the New York to Paris race around the world. However, the railroads competed in what was most assuredly the harder and more expensive race.

The two newest Great Northern workers got off to an early start, and began working on the road building through the Dakotas at a very fast pace. However, the GN surveyors had laid out the northernmost route and faced some big obstacles in the form of mountains ahead of them. In fact, they were forced to dig out more "cuts" along mountainsides and dig more tunnels than they would have wished to. The route that paralleled that of the Great Northern was laid out by the Northern Pacific, and the route to the south of the NP's was the one selected by the Milwaukee Road. The latter two routes came together at Bozeman Pass, through the Bridger Mountains in Montana, which had been named for the mountain man and explorer Jim Bridger.

Since the N.P. was headed directly for Seattle in a race with the Great Northern, and the Milwaukee Road was headed for Portland, they agreed to use the route through the pass and into Bozeman, Montana that both lines would share. Their "Freight Houses," built for handling less-than-carload consignments of freight, sit across the street from each other on Main Street in Bozeman, Montana and both are still standing there, but put to other uses.

It was late November by the time the GN and the two Boomers reached Spokane, Washington. The railroad's managers decided they were not going to try to push the line through the Cascade mountain range that Winter so they laid all of their construction crew workers off. Archie was offered continued employment, but Ed was not. Archie said they should just keep heading West together.

Neither of the other two competing railroads had reached Spokane yet, however the Spokane, Portland & Seattle Railroad originated there (as their name implied). Both men were eager to reach the coast, so they decided to temporarily give up being boomers and buy tickets for passage on the S.P.&S. to Portland. The route of the S.P.&S. took them through the beautiful Columbia River Gorge.

Columbia River Gorge

When the two arrived in Portland, they learned that the Southern Pacific Railroad was hiring men to work in their large, railroad-repair shops in Roseville, California, to the East of Sacramento. The S.P. shops were huge and the railroad even built some of their own steam locomotives there, including their famous cab-forward engine. The two men worked hard for the S.P. in those shops after they decided to quit being boomers.

As provided in the Homestead Act of 1862, up to 160 acres of free land was available to each man for only a small filing fee. Ed and Archie decided to homestead some grassland, Northeast of Sacramento, adjacent to one another. This gave them a combined 320 acres, which was a decent amount of acreage for raising "feeder calves" for the nearby markets in the city.

Even though the joint venture into the cattle feeding business was very successful, Archie was a "restless" rancher. He decided to sell his share of the land and small herd to Ed, and he moved to San Francisco to open up a blacksmith shop about four blocks South of the busy intersection of Market and California Streets,

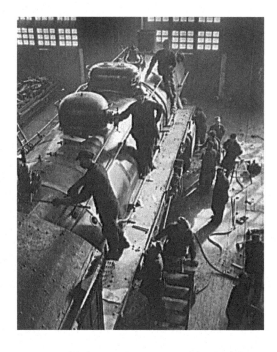

where the Hyatt Regency Hotel now stands, across the street from the old brick headquarters of the Southern Pacific Railroad, the last railroad the two boomers worked for. When he retired, many years later, Archie sold his shop and, in recent times, was operated by a man named Edwin Klockars.

Ed continued to work in the S.P. shops in Roseville and hired a young man to tend the ranch. He worked for the S.P. for many years, then retired and lived the rest of his days in comfort in a small town located half a dozen miles east of Roseville. The town was named Newcastle, which was ironic, because the city just North of his birthplace in Sunderland, England, was named Newcastle—a bustling, coal-mining area and shipbuilding center—the place it was said nobody would ship coal to. There was an old saying that any useless activity was "like shipping coal to Newcastle."

When he moved to Newcastle, Ed found a small, white, clapboard house and had a glassed-in porch added to it and planted palms and hibiscus plants in pots—just like Uncle Bob's porch that he had admired so.

Archie and Bob remained lifelong friends and visited each other often. Neither of them married and the Shanks name ended when Ed expired. His brother George perished at sea in the First World War and had not married his childhood sweetheart before enlisting.

10 ❖ They Called Him Ishi

The Last of the Yahi

Although it was not his real name, he was called Ishi, and he was the last living member of a small tribe of four hundred or so Native Americans who had called themselves the Yahi. They were hunter-gatherers, who subsisted in a rugged landscape in Northern California that lay East of the town of Oroville. The land was filled with steep cliffs, deep valleys and streams that flowed down the steep slopes of the volcanic Mount Lassen to the North. The Yahi's territory, which they did not claim to own because the concept of ownership of the land was foreign to them, was mostly covered with dense thickets of manzanita brush, tall ponderosa pine and scrubby live oak trees.

The majority of the Yahi people were small in stature, due to a sparse diet of venison, fry bread made with acorn meal, grass seed cakes, roots and wild berries in the Spring. They were, however, a very aggressive tribe when it came to defending their tiny territory from encroachment by other tribes, and later from the White men who came to find those pebbles that shone like the sun.

After White market hunters and gold-seekers had killed off most of the coastal blacktail deer, the Yahi started killing cattle and stealing food from nearby cattle ranches. Of course, this angered the ranchers, who retaliated by shooting and killing any Yahi they found in the vicinity.

Also, ever since the California Gold Rush days, any Natives who had not adopted the White man's ways and clothing were considered to be "hostiles" and fair game for many a white man with a rifle or pistol.

In fact, at that time, the Government of the State of California was paying a bounty to the State Militia and groups of Vigilantes for any scalps of the "hostiles," and an even higher bounty was paid for their heads. It was said that some scalps from murdered Mexicans were even being passed off as those taken from Natives.

By 1871, over three-fourths of the entire Yahi tribe had been killed by the Whites. After that, groups of thirty-to-forty of the remaining survivors were being pursued and pushed into their hiding places only to be massacred by vigilantes. One of the killers said he could not shoot young Yahi children with his rifle, claiming it made too much mess. So, he killed them with his pistol instead. The very last massacre of the Yahi was in 1908, when all but three of the tribe were killed. The three members of the small family were able to escape by playing dead and floating downstream among the dead bodies of the others. They were able to survive for more than a year by living in a cave at the foot of a high cliff at a location they called "the bear's hiding place."

One cold November day, a group of three surveyors discovered the cave, and the family fled in fear for their lives. After the three Natives were gone, the surveyors took everything that the three needed to survive the coming Winter as trophies.

The Last Resort

It was February, and near midnight, the meadow was illuminated by a full moon surrounded by a halo of ice crystals. The ground was totally covered with a thick rime of hoarfrost and wet snow that had fallen much earlier that evening. A storm had carried moisture-laden clouds driven by a cold, North wind all the way down the West Coast from the Straits of Georgia, located between the mainland of British Columbia and Vancouver Island. When the saturated mass of cold air rose over the tops of the Siskiyou Mountain range, located to the North of Mount Lassen, it reached its dew point and huge wet snowflakes blanketed the Northern California landscape from the Oregon border all the way to the capital city of Sacramento.

The outer branches of the sagebrush growing in the meadow were weighed down with a coating of ice and snow. The shapes of their limbs reminded Ishi of the outstretched arms of the dying members of the Yahi tribe. Ishi was angered by the memory, however his rising anger did nothing to help warm him. He drew the tattered remnants of a ragged deerskin closer around his shoulders, but the thin hide didn't do much to alleviate the bitter cold. Aside from that small covering, his body was naked from his torso on down, and he no longer had any feeling in his feet as he dragged them across the frozen soil.

The deerskin that Ishi clutched across his chest with his right hand was taken from the last small deer he had killed with his bow and arrows, which had been left, along with all of the other possessions his family had to abandon at the bear's hiding place. In his left hand, he clutched his handmade knife that his mother had used to shave the hair off that same bear skin that she intended to use to make them some new moccasins. Ishi had fashioned the weapon years ago, and it was the first of many of the finest knives that the members of the Yahi tribe had ever seen.

He treasured this knife—his last remaining possession from the days of his youth. The day it was made, he'd been hunting far North of the tribe's usual hunting grounds with the hope of finding one of the groups of migratory mule deer that descend from the high mountains each Winter to live at lower elevations.

Mule deer were usually much larger than any black-tails. Finding and killing one would guarantee him a reputation as a great hunter. So concentrated on finding and killing a mule deer was Ishi that he had not given much thought to the amount of work it would take to carry a carcass almost as heavy as himself the many miles back to the tribe.

As he walked silently through a grove of live oak trees, Ishi thought he could make out a faint chipping noise up ahead. When he exited the grove, he spied a man that he did not recognize squatting down ahead. He was from another tribe!

The man signed that he was friendly and was from the much larger Yana tribe that lived in the lands just North of the Yahi. He was a toolmaker and the arrowheads at his feet were the finest Ishi had ever seen. Not one of the Yahi toolmakers had the artistry this man clearly possessed. The interest Ishi showed in the man's work led the toolmaker to demonstrate how he chipped the intricate shapes and sharp edges of arrowheads with the larger stone he held in his left hand. Ishi signed that he would like to try to make a tool, and the toolmaker grinned with approval as he gave Ishi a piece of dark obsidian (greenish-black, volcanic glass) and his stone chipper. He then drew the shape of a knife on the ground.

It was many hours later when Ishi finally had learned some of the techniques that the man was teaching him and had completed his first knife. It was the first of many that he would make for himself and for other Yahi men and women, and he'd become the tribe's toolmaker rather than the great hunter he envisioned himself someday becoming.

Right now, the cold was not the biggest problem Ishi faced. He was starving! Ever since he, his mother, and his sister had fled their home in the cave at the bear's hiding place, they had been living on a meager diet of cattail roots and hibernating ground squirrels that they were able to dig out of their holes in the ground. The last thing they had eaten was a soup made from boiled strips of the hide that Ishi now had wrapped around his shoulders.

Last week his mother had died, and this morning he was unable to wake his little sister from a coma-like sleep. He was sure that even if he was successful in his attempt to secure some food, the young woman would be dead when he returned with it. But where was he going to find anything to eat?

His only hope would be to head toward the town of Oroville. If he was lucky, he might find a milk cow with a nursing calf that he could slay with his knife. Since it was the middle of Winter, all of the beef cattle in the area had either already been slaughtered or shipped away to feedlots.

After Ishi crossed the two shiny tracks that the fire-breathing wagon always used to travel up and down the valley, he approached the log enclosures where many head of beef cattle were held before they were loaded inside the wooden pens on wheels that the fire-wagon pulled in a long line behind it. There were no cattle outside, but Ishi could smell fresh meat coming from inside the structure adjacent to the pens.

This place was the Oroville slaughterhouse, and there was a ramp that led into the side of the building that Ishi used to enter. Deep inside the building Ishi found many beef carcasses hanging on hooks, and he began cutting off thin strips of meat and devouring them. The meat was not as moist and flavorful as the deer meat he was used to eating, but he believed it might sustain him for at least another week. He knew that he would not be able to stay very long in the slaughterhouse, because he had observed that there were White men who arrived there each morning to work. But he also knew that if he had to leave the town of Oroville, he had no inkling how he might be able to survive.

It was a bit warmer inside than it was outdoors, so Ishi decided he would squat down in a back corner of the building until dawn. He dared not sleep for fear of being discovered when the White men arrived, so he began to think back to when the killing of the Yahi tribe first started. He had been out looking for some obsidian not far from the place the Yahi spent each Summer, when he heard the first volley of shots and the anguished cries of the wounded. His mother and sister were close by gathering edible seeds, and the three of them headed North toward where some other members of the tribe had gone to gather acorns.

They failed to locate the group of Yahi they were looking for, but Ishi spied the Yana toolmaker digging in the sand near the foot of a bluff. The two had spent enough time together that they'd learned enough of their very similar dialects. Ishi politely asked what the man was doing; since it was obvious the sand there contained no obsidian. The toolmaker replied that he was retrieving buried weapons. The Yana had learned about the ongoing slaughter of many of the Native populations to the South and they were planning on relocating far to the Northeast. Last Fall, a small group of the Shoshone tribe from Idaho had passed through the area mounted on beautiful dappled horses. They had explained they were on their annual migration South to the valley where the Washoe and Paiute tribes wintered each year.

Both of these tribes co-existed peacefully in the same valley each Winter, hunting duck and geese, and fishing in the river flowing from the lake in the hills where the Washoe caught and lived on fish each Summer. Since the two tribes shared their Winter grounds, it was possible that the elders of the Shoshone, a peaceful people, might also be willing to share their much larger territory in Idaho with the Yana.

The Yana were given the directions to travel to the Shoshone territory by heading East over Deer Creek pass, then North past the Modoc tribe's lava rock-filled territory, then Northeast following the great shining river that flowed from Canada to the sea. After they reached the Snake River, the Yana people were to follow it upstream, past the tribes of fish-eaters whose camps reeked of fish offal, until they reached the falls in the deep gorge.

The Shoshone man warned them not to travel further East into the territory of the Blackfeet who were said to hate everyone who was not a Blackfoot, and who would undoubtedly slay all of the Yana men and make slaves of the women. The elder toolmaker begged

Ishi not to share the Yana's plans for migration with any of the Yahi tribe leaders, because only the Yana Tribe had been given permission by the Shoshone to come to Idaho.

Into the World of the White Man

After recalling that day, Ishi had fallen asleep and was awakened by the barking of a dog that had quickly scented him and given alarm to two men following the hound into the slaughterhouse.

When they spied Ishi, who was cowering in the corner, they exclaimed, "My God, it's a wild man!"

Nearly naked, he did indeed look the part of a wild man. His skin was quite dark, and his hair was singed down to his scalp. He had burned it himself, when he was mourning the death of his mother.

Ishi was then covered with a canvas tarp and taken to the Tehama County Sheriff, who quickly

decided to lock him up for safekeeping. The Sheriff then notified a local newspaper editor about the capture of a nearly naked, wild man. Soon, both the Oroville and San Francisco papers told the story of the wild man who had wandered into Oroville from the forests near Deer Creek.

Doctor Alfred L. Kroeber, an Anthropologist at the University of California at Berkeley, had an on-going desire to study an American aboriginal people and their culture as it existed before it was exposed to the White men. Dr. Kroeber desperately wanted to meet and study this so-called wild man who, he thought, just might be a true aboriginal. Kroeber had other responsibilities at the time, so he sent his colleague, Mister T.T. Waterman, to Oroville to meet and bring the Yahi to Berkeley for study.

After he arrived, Waterman found someone had dressed the captive in a shirt and pants, but he was not wearing any shoes. The man's feet were nearly as wide as they were long, and he was not able to tolerate having them enclosed in the widest shoes found in Oroville. It was obvious that they would have to have a boot maker custom-make a pair with the softest leather for the native. Waterman had little trouble convincing the sheriff to turn his captive over to him.

The two men traveled South by train. The members of the Yahi tribe had observed and heard trains from a distance, but had never seen how they traveled over the two shiny steel rails. The huge and deafening steam locomotives belched smoke. This, and the loud wails of their steam whistles, convinced the Yahi tribe that the huge machines were powered by demons that the White man had somehow managed to confine inside the black tubes in front of the cabs.

The speed of the train on the long ride South was exhilarating for Ishi, and there was an equally exciting ride on a steam-powered ferryboat that took them across the Carquinez Strait located at the North end of the San Francisco Bay. The most water the Yahi people had ever seen was in the streams that were filled up to the top of their banks after the Winter and Spring rains fell on the hilly land they lived in east of Oroville.

Here was a huge river that flowed into a great body of water! Also, this water had a faint fishy smell, and Ishi could taste salt on the tiny amount of spray

that formed on his lips as he stood outside and faced the wind and looked toward the bow as the ferry rapidly made it's way toward the shore.

None of the Yahi had any idea that there were so many White people living in California, and Ishi was amazed when he saw the crowds of White men and women, who were all dressed in their many layers of clothing, walking along the flat, hard paths next to the roads of San Francisco and Berkeley.

When Kroeber first met the Yahi man, he made an attempt to communicate with him by using the sign language of the Pomo Indians he had studied. This was a complete failure. Although many of the North American native tribes had developed a simple kind of sign language that they could each use when they interacted or conducted trading with other tribes, the Yahi were truly an isolated tribe that had never interacted with other peoples, except the nearby Yana.

When Ishi spoke, his words were like none that Kroeber had ever heard uttered by any of the northern California Native Americans he had met with and studied. The only Yahi word Kroeber thought he comprehended was Ishi, which he assumed was the Yahi's name. Actually, Ishi was the Yahi word for man, but from that day forward he was going to be called Ishi by all. Ishi's true name was never revealed since, according to Yahi culture, you only used your own name with others in the tribe and never told anyone else you might chance to meet what it was. This may have been related to the idea of some Native Americans who always refused to have their picture taken, fearing that it might rob them of part of their soul.

Another Native American who made attempts to communicate with Ishi was called Sam Batwai *(Bat-why)*. However, Batwai was also unsuccessful. Moreover, Ishi did not care for the man, who looked down on Ishi because he had not been assimilated into the White culture as he had.

Kroeber gave Ishi a room in the University's Cultural Museum and paid him a small salary for doing some of the janitorial duties. The many Native American artifacts stored there were fascinating to Ishi. Then, after he had learned to speak some English, Ishi informed Kroeber that one of the willow baskets he'd seen in the collection was actually one that his mother had woven. That was most likely true, since the surveyors who had taken all of their belongings from the cave later sold them to Kroeber for display in the University Museum. In addition to the basket, Ishi found several other items that had once belonged to his family.

A Return to the Land of the Yahi

Eventually, the Bureau of Indian affairs offered Ishi an opportunity to live on an Indian Reservation and become an honorary member of the Blackfoot tribe. He quickly declined the offer and decided to remain at the University, where he was content.

Ishi and T.T. Waterman amused themselves with target practice with bow and arrows, and even though he was a good hunter with his handmade bow and arrows, Waterman proved to be a better marksman with his. Also, Ishi lacked any incentive to shoot at man-made targets and said he much preferred to shoot his arrows when hunting for live animals.

That Summer, Kroeber was able to persuade Ishi to accompany him on a camping trip to the Yahi territory to demonstrate the hunting techniques his tribe had used when they lived off the land.

After numerous requests, Ishi finally agreed to take Doctor Kroeber to visit the cave at the bear's hiding place. Ishi was visibly moved and saddened when he recalled the narrow escape from the vigilantes and the resulting death of his mother and sister.

Ishi was a big attraction at the University Museum. Kroeber was offered a sizeable donation if he would permit Ishi to travel with a sideshow, but he quickly declined. Ishi did enjoy going to Golden Gate Park to visit the zoo and interact with the crowds of interested members of the public. He also made an exhibit there by building a Yahi dwelling with sticks. He became quite disturbed when a group of boisterous children started to tear it apart, and he ran and chased them off. Otherwise, he was a calm and friendly person.

Kroeber was able to find a linguistic expert, Edward Siphere *(Ci-fear)*, a Canadian who specialized in the study of many Native American languages, including those of the Yana tribe, who lived in close proximity to the Yahi. Siphere believed that by working closely with Ishi, could interpret his speech patterns. He recorded them on wax cylinders hoping that he might be able to make a glossary of Yahi words. Unfortunately, there had been very little contact between the Yana and Yahi tribes, and none of the Yana words were remotely similar to Yahi words. The Yahi language was always a great mystery to the members of the Yana tribe.

All of the laborious recordings were made on Ediphone wax cylinders, and the numerous interpretation sessions took an extremely long time. It was necessary for Ishi to first gain a very rudimentary understanding of English in order for him to explain what each Yahi word meant. Edward was finally able to learn enough of the Yahi language to fully translate Ishi's recording of a quite humorous folk tale about a wood duck and various other forest creatures that Ishi recorded using different tones for the voices of each.

Dr. Alfred Kroeber with Ishi

The entire process took countless hours and this took a toll on the health of Ishi, who had never been exposed to any of the diseases the White people carried. Ishi fell ill. A Berkeley physician, Doctor Saxton Pope, treated him for a serious illness and Ishi later became a close friend of the Pope family.

Ishi was eventually hospitalized again for quite a long period, but after his condition improved somewhat, Dr. Pope gave him a guided tour of the hospital. Ishi was shocked to see some of the University Medical

School's students engaged in the process of dissecting cadavers, and he was quite horrified by the idea that this was what the White people did with their dead.

Kroeber was studying in Europe when he received a telegram that advised him that Ishi's condition had worsened, and that he had died from tuberculosis. Kroeber wrote Doctor Pope a reply with detailed instructions for handling the remains and a burial, and insisted that no autopsy be performed.

In fact, his letter stated, "If there is any talk of the interests of science, then say for me that science can go to hell." Regretfully, Kroeber's letter arrived after the autopsy was already done and Ishi's brain had been removed for study.

Like all of the Yahi people, Ishi surely believed the legend that told them when they died their soul flew to the South and entered a hole in the earth. It is possible this Doctor Kroeber might have been comforted by the thought that, as the Native man he had had studied and considered his friend was taking his last breath, his final thought was that his soul would make its way to that final resting place.

❖ Epilogue

The Western half of the United States has always held a great attraction for those who wanted to trap, hunt, mine, or log its treasure trove of great resources. Some wanted to grow crops that are difficult to grow—or to grow them better than the place they were living at the time. As depicted in these stories based on history, they came from all parts of the globe.

Not long after the first settlers arrived on the East Coast of what is now the United States, many of those same immigrants had a strong inclination to continue moving in a westward direction in their desire for new lands to settle. In the mid 1800s this migration was termed "manifest destiny."

This belief actually maintained that this expansive land was destined—by whom, God?—to be exploited by those who came here from England, Ireland and Western Europe to take, by force if necessary, all of the land that was then occupied solely by a vast population of Natives and Spaniards.

The lure of the open lands to the West led a great number of people to embark on journeys that could be, and usually were, very difficult for all who decided to undertake that migration, and lives and fortunes were often lost as a result. However, that great movement of "settlers" to the West proved to be infinitely harder on those who were already inhabiting those lands.

What actually took place during the settlement of the West is hardly what I first read about as a youngster in Edison Grade School in the early 1940s. In fact, the more that I later read and learned about that subject as an adult, the darker the history revealed itself to be. Every one of us boys who chose to play "cowboys and indians" in those days had no clue about the actual history behind the exciting stories that were portrayed for us by Hollywood.

Of course, there was a lot of bloodshed back then. Any number of some, but hardly all, of the atrocities on both sides were depicted. But the Native peoples who were fighting in a futile attempt to defend their way of life were almost always portrayed as "the bad guys" in the majority of those exciting "westerns" we watched on those Saturday afternoons.

Finally, the great multitude of Nature's bounty is no doubt the reason behind why there was such a large number of Native American tribes—now more accurately described as "First People" by Canadians—who occupied what is now the State of California at the time the Spanish Missionaries arrived. Those good Christians were, no doubt, fervently convinced that by "converting" many of the Natives to be loyal Catholic subjects, they were doing them a great service. Of course, the fact that they often required those same converted subjects to serve the Church by doing hard labor is sometimes overlooked.

So, in the writer's opinion, the treatment, conversion, and very often the genocide, of many of those Native Americans, by a fair number of the White men who later came to the West, can only be accurately described as deplorable.

If the reader has any doubts about this, he or she should refer to Wikipedia's list of Indian massacres. Although the term Indian Massacres was first used to describe attacks by tribes of Native Americans upon the settlements and forts occupied by Whites, it was later used to describe the attacks upon and the genocide of the Native peoples. The most famous of these are the Sand Creek and Wounded Knee Massacres, close to the end of the so-called Indian Wars in the late 1860s.

The total number of deaths of both the Whites and Natives from massacres that occurred during those years is roughly 29,000 Natives and 9,000 Whites. The total number of Natives killed is an extremely rough estimate because the native deaths were often reported in ranges like 100-to-400, 300-to-1,000, and 200-to-1200. Even the total number of dead Native men, women and children buried in a mass grave at Wounded Knee has been reported as ranging from 130 to 250.

One of the last of the pursuits of hostiles (those being native Americans who resisted surrendering their lands and being confined on a reservation) was conducted by troops commanded by General Howard against the Nez Perce tribe, led by Chief Joseph. This action was termed the Nez Perce war of 1877.

After the Nez Perce were pursued over 1,170 miles across five states, and 150 of their tribe, numbering 450, were killed, Chief Joseph formally surrendered to General Miles on the afternoon of October 5th, 1877. The words attributed to Joseph at the formal surrender are a part of the history of the settlement of the West:

"IT DOES NOT REQUIRE MANY WORDS TO SPEAK THE TRUTH."
CHIEF JOSEPH, NEZ PERCE TRIBE

Tell General Howard I know his heart. What he told me before I have it in my heart. I am tired of fighting. Our chiefs are killed. Looking Glass is dead. 'Too-hul-hul-sote' is dead. The old men are all dead. It is the young men who say yes or no. He who led on the young men is dead. It is cold, and we have no blankets. The little children are freezing to death. My people, some of them, have run away to the hills, and have no blankets, no food. No one knows where they are—perhaps freezing to death. I want to have time to look for my children, to see how many I can find. Maybe I shall find them among the dead. Hear me, my chiefs! I am tired. My heart is sick and sad. From where the sun now stands, I will fight no more forever.

The tribe was moved from one to another reservation and ended up in Oklahoma, a long way from their beloved land in Oregon. In his later years, Joseph spoke eloquently against the United States Government's policy toward his people and hoped America's promise of freedom and equality might one day be fulfilled for our Native Americans as well.

❖ *The Mustang*

EXCERPT FROM *WALKING WITH MUSTANGS & OTHER WILD ANIMAL TALES*

To look at him, most would bet a good sum that he was a purebred Arabian stallion. You could tell that by the shape of his head, the pale, ghostlike body coloring, the black dusting around his narrow nose and large nostrils, and the flowing black mane and tail. He was really a mustang, a mixed breed, although his appearance would lead one to believe otherwise.

Mustangs roam free on unfenced (usually public) lands and aren't domesticated, but unlike most other wild animals, when given the right opportunity, they can bond with humans. They respond quite readily to gentleness, as opposed to heavy-handed methods of "breaking them in." So, their scientific description of Equus ferus—feral horse—is the more accurate term.

Mustangs usually have a mixture of genes (or DNA) from many horses, and the variety of sizes, bone structures and colors are endless. It was unusual to see the typical coloring and traits of a purebred Arabian in a mustang. Was this a domesticated animal that was set free to wander? Even if this was the case, his DNA might be traced back to the time when horses were brought to North America by the first legions of Spanish Conquistadors, or years later, when officers Santa Ana at The Alamo were felled by accompanying well-aimed ball shot from Kentucky rifles and their horses ran off into the surrounding countryside.

So, what was this striking mustang doing here, alone in the Yukon Territory, after possibly being driven from his herd by a stronger stallion eager to lessen competition for brood mares? Did he travel many miles North, following the sun as it moved each Spring from Northern Alberta to the territory where he found lots of new growth of tender, spring grasses?

Or was he following some primal urge to travel toward the land bridge across the Bering Straits, just as the ancient herds did when they migrated across this territory and were bound for new homes in the steppes of what is now Russia? Recently some Paleontologists have identified jawbones of small horses found in the Yukon Territory that were thousands of years old, but no herds of feral horses are found there today.

In any case, if he found no herds to join up with, he just might be searching for a man, because by nature horses were herd animals that always had the urge to "join up" with others for protection, And, of course, the Yukon Territory was home to numerous species of predatory animals, so this urge would be an extremely strong one.

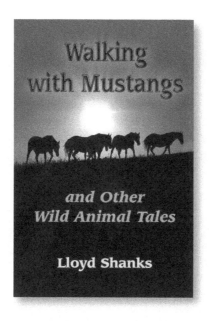

Walking with Mustangs & Other Wild Animal Tales
is available on Amazon.com

Autographed copies of
They Came to the West
may be purchased for $16.95 + $3 postage.
Contact the author by email at: muledeerpress@gmail.com
or by postal mail to:
MULE DEER PRESS
3426 Lemhi Trail Drive • Bozeman, Montana 59718
Also available on Amazon.com

❖ *About the Author*

L loyd Shanks has always been an avid reader and also enjoys writing. In 1946, at the age of eleven, he traveled by himself from Chicago to Sacramento on a steam-powered passenger train and then lived on a boarding ranch and attended a one-room school in Calaveras County, California. This ranch was located in the very heart of the historic "Gold Country."

As a teenager, he visited many of the towns in the foothills of the Sierras. He and his friends visited communities with colorful names like Angels Camp, San Andreas, Placerville, Railroad Flat, Chinese Camp, Volcano, Mokelumne Hill and Fiddletown. They explored the remains of many old mining sites and swam in some deep pools in the Mokelumne River near tall piles of rock deposited by gold dredges.

As an adult, he and his wife Gerrianne drove over the rutted one-lane road between Copperopolis and Milton, where Black Bart was said to have committed his first stagecoach robbery, and they stayed overnight at a haunted mansion in Coloma, the site of John Marshall's discovery of gold in 1848. Over the years, he has held a deep fascination for the West and stories about those who immigrated there in the 1800s.

They Came to the West is a product of Lloyd's version of "gold fever," which has been honed over the years of reading other tales of the West, such as those written by Samuel Clements (pen name Mark Twain) and Brett Harte, and numerous books about the Donner Party, the most recent being an excellent account found in *The Donner Party Chronicles,* by Frank Mullen Jr.